SON OF

FILM FLUBS™

More Memorable Movie Mistakes

by Bill Givens

A Citadel Press Book
Published by Carol Publishing Group

10 9 8 7 6 5 4 3 2 1

Film Flubs™ and Son of Film Flubs™ are registered trademarks of Bill Givens.

Library of Congress Cataloging-in-Publication Data

Givens, Bill
    Son of film flubs : more memorable movie mistakes / by Bill
Givens.
      p. cm.
   "A Citadel Press book."
   ISBN 0-8065-1279-2
    1. Motion pictures—Humor. 2. Motion pictures—Anecdotes.
I. Title.
PN1994.9.G59   1991
791.43'75'0207—dc20
                            91-33765
                            CIP

Dedicated to the script supervisors, editors, directors, costume and prop crews, camera crews, and all of the other professionals in the motion picture industry who not only enrich our lives with their work, but have been so generous in letting us have a smile or a laugh at their own expense as we reveal the little foibles in the greatest entertainment medium of them all.

And for Reed, Janie, Rob, Jon, and MaryRea.

CONTENTS

ACKNOWLEDGMENTS

This book exists because so many people made its predecessor, *FILM FLUBS,* a success—creating a *raison d'etre* for *SON OF FILM FLUBS.* A special thanks to agent, author, and friend Bart Andrews for advice, counsel, and support; to Gail Kinn, Alvin H. Marill, Jessica Black, Ben Petrone, and all of the staff at Carol Publishing Group; Heather Vincent and Judy Muller of *ABC World News Tonight with Peter Jennings;* Ann Ruddy of *The Entertainment Report;* Leonard Maltin, Ben Herndon, and Glenn Meehan of *Entertainment Tonight;* Dan Weaver and Geraldo Rivera of *Geraldo;* Steve Proffit and Eric Engberg of *CBS Nightwatch;* the staff of *Cinemax Movie News;* Brad Hurtado of Detroit's WXYZ-TV who was so kind to a "green" author; and all of the national media who were so kind and generous in spreading the word about *FILM FLUBS.* A special thanks is reserved for Susan Wloszczyna of *USA Today,* whose wonderful article on the book spurred a flood of letters, providing much of the fodder for *SON OF FILM FLUBS;* Ryan Murphy, whose syndicated *Miami Herald* piece kicked off a torrent of publicity; and Copley Radio Network for their "Flash Bulletin" that unleashed a flash flood of radio and television interviews.

We've discovered that the media is full of film buffs, and it's been a real delight to talk with writers, newscasters, and talk show hosts around the nation, as well as to the hundreds of film fans who called in to the shows to talk about their favorite flubs. Hopefully, the ones you told us about are included herein; if not, look for them in a future volume.

Once again, we owe a deep debt of gratitude to the staff of the Margaret Herrick Library of the Academy of Motion Picture Arts and Sciences, now happily ensconced in their "waterworks palace," and to the staff of the American Film Institute Library. The guys at Video West in Studio City as always were extremely helpful in digging out the tapes we needed to verify flubs, as well as pitching in a few of their favorites. And thanks to Cinema Collectors, Hollywood Book & Poster, Larry Edmonds Bookshop, and especially the staff of Collectors Book Store for adding a bit of fun to the tedious search for movie stills.

Special gratitude for encouragement and support to Terri Minsky, Ken Bostic, Craig Phillips, the Gottfrieds, Rosebud "not-a-sled" Davis, and many, many friends who've made the hard work that goes into writing a book a rewarding experience.

Bill Givens

June 1991

HOW DO THEY HAPPEN?

Whenever the topic of movie continuity errors arises, two questions invariably come up. The first is "How do these things happen?" The second: "Whose job is it to catch them?"

There's no one single answer to the first question. Historical errors and slips of logic happen because no one noticed (sloppy research, perhaps), usually in the script stage but sometimes on the set. Mismatches happen because the movement of a prop or a minute change in an actor's costume went unnoticed, but more often they are an unfortunate result of the editing process. Things appear odd at times because film must (1) be flipped to maintain screen direction or (2) run backwards to make a special effect work.

As to the second question, there's really no one person to whom a finger can be pointed. It's the job of each craft involved with a film to maintain, if you will, the "purity" of their work as it appears on screen. The prop builders must make sure that hand props are authentic and operate properly; the on-set prop people are responsible for the props being in the right place throughout each day's filming. Likewise the costumers must be certain that their work is true to period. Dressers make sure that such things as a collar remain buttoned (or unbuttoned), but actors open the buttons between takes for comfort, and sometimes no one notices the difference until the scene's frozen in time on film.

On the set, the overall responsibility for keeping things kosher falls on the shoulders of the script supervisor. There are some things that slip by, others that can't be changed, still more that happen in the post-production process, when it's pretty much out of the script supervisor's hands. Ultimately, it's the director's picture—but unless he has what Hollywood calls "final cut" (read: the absolute last word before the work is unleashed to the masses), things can get away from him, too.

Shortly after *FILM FLUBS* was published, we took a look at the blockbuster hit *Pretty Woman* and, noting five or six continuity errors, nominated it for the FLUBBIE Award for "Flubbed-Up Movie of the Year." Recently, we had occasion to talk about the film with its script supervisor, a lovely lady named Adell Aldrich. Ms. Aldrich has a long career as a script supervisor. Her first job was at the age of sixteen, supervising script on a classic film, *Whatever Happened to Baby Jane?* (1962). The film was by one of Hollywood's great directors—her father, Robert Aldrich.

Pretty Woman (1990), directed by Garry Marshall, was chosen for the FLUBBIE because of a series of onscreen mismatches:

(1) When Julia Roberts is undressing Richard Gere, she takes off his tie, then unbuttons his shirt. There's a reaction shot from Gere, and he's wearing the tie.

7

(2) When they're having breakfast, Julia picks up a croissant, but takes a bite from a pancake. And the bite that was taken from the pancake is restored in the next shot.

(3) Gere is playing the piano in one sequence in a near-empty ballroom. In one shot, a chair behind him is empty; in the next, there's a man sitting in it.

(4) When they're having a picnic in the park, Julia takes off Gere's shoes and socks. In the next shot, they're inexplicably back on.

(5) When the two are having dinner at a fancy restaurant with Ralph Bellamy, Gere's sorbet dish vanishes before your eyes, then reappears.

We should first point out that no, we didn't cause Ms. Aldrich to lose work because of the notoriety we gave to the film's mismatches. She frequently works with Garry Marshall on his films as well as many others and says that she keeps a copy of the "Flubbie" article in her script book. "I wave it in his face if he starts to mismatch," she laughs. "Sometimes outsiders ask me about it, but not people in the business. They know how these things happen."

Each of the errors we spotted in *Pretty Woman*, she says, was the result of editing cuts. "When you get a story that's really long, they start taking out middles of scenes, cutting speeches and stories. That's how you go, for example, from croissant to pancake." The "tie" mismatch, she says, is the result of the editor needing a transition scene to keep a cut from "jumping" (when two similar shots are cut together from the same scene, there will be a jarring jump unless another shot is inserted in the middle of the cut). It was the only shot available from that scene. In fact, it appears that there was an attempt to optically crop it to minimize the appearance of the tie.

The situation with the picnic scene was similar—there was dialogue wherein he put the shoes back on, but it was cut in the final edit. Thus the mismatch. And as for the sorbet scene: "There was a whole scene with Bellamy, entire speeches that were cut out."

Pretty Woman is, like so many movies, far from the film as originally conceived. As written, there was a drug use subplot and a much darker ending with Gere abandoning Roberts, returning her to her street life. Once studio executives issued their notes (and Disney—a.k.a. Touchstone—is famous for its barrages of studio notes), the film changed directions entirely.

Into the mix you put the work habits of the director. Some shoot lean—pretty much shooting scene to scene with little extra footage, little improvisation on the set, few changes. Others let the actors have their say, try new things, and shoot considerable "coverage"—additional angles on the same scene, to enliven the editing process and add visual interest. *Pretty Woman*'s Garry Marshall falls into the latter category.

"With Garry, every first cut is four hours," Aldrich says. "He has a lot of dialogue that wasn't written into the script that surrounds the scene or is the middle of scenes. He invents a lot of it as he goes, so he ends up with four-hour movies. But we know that the studio isn't going to release a four-hour movie, so two hours have to get cut. I think that's where his genius is—in cutting it down and making it a strong story."

She points out that two or three people check and double-check each other's work in the process of making a film. "When things are really blatant, you know that it can't be the script supervisor. It has to be something that they did in the post production process—juxtaposing scenes, cutting out middles, things like that.

"Prop guys and set guys are responsible for the physical props and the wardrobe guys are responsible for matching the wardrobe. The hair people are responsible for sending them back to the set with the same hairstyle. There's such a check and balance system, and there's always the film to go look at if you really don't know which door they came in or what was in their hands. It's rare to have such blatant mistakes. Ultimately, yes, I'm responsible. But it takes two or three people not doing their jobs before it gets to me. It's pretty hard to make blatant mistakes."

And sometimes there's just nothing that can be done, even when she knows that something's awry. Having recently finished working on a major film about much that has been written in regard to its behind-the-scenes mayhem, she names an actress and adds that "you couldn't get her to do the same thing twice. But your coworkers and those who hire you know that."

Ms. Aldrich adds that the script supervisor develops a trained eye, a photographic memory, and a "sixth sense" about the way things should be.

"You look for watches, wardrobe things, books on a coffee table, things like that. You're basically responsible for it all. After a while, your eye will go directly to what's wrong. You photograph it in your mind, or you take pictures. I don't use pictures any more. I just walk in and tell you what's wrong. My kids were amazed that I could walk into the house and literally tell them what they'd been doing all day. They never could figure it out."

Another area on which we agree heartily is a situation in Hollywood that builds in the possibility of onscreen error. It has to do with the way things operate today. Films are put together and frequently shown to those damnable "focus groups" or taken to previews out in the hustings, and comment cards from the audience sometimes convince the studios to cut scenes or change endings.

"It's not like it used to be," she points out. It's a science putting them together now. They go out and test films, put them through all these exercises, want more laughter, want more sex, want more gunshots. The editing process is different."

What she's saying is that scenes are often reshot to change or add or cut things after the original film is wrapped and edited to make it into a marketable product. Show business is, after all, a business.

"Before, a filmmaker literally gave you his vision. All the good directors did it that way. They didn't have to answer to twelve people at a studio, to the corporation that owns the corporation. They went in and shook Harry Cohn's hand and they made a movie. We don't have that system in Hollywood anymore. Some of these studio people don't know what a camera is, don't know what a crane is, don't know what a grip is. They come from business backgrounds. They're not filmmakers. I come from old Hollywood. I hate to see it go."

As long as there are professionals like Adell Aldrich who really care about movies, who do their work so well, and who are such good sports that they can take a few good-natured jibes from *FILM FLUBS*, Hollywood just might recover.

TITLE TROUBLES

It's really tough when you find that you can't even trust the title of a movie. After all, the title is supposed to give you at least a vague idea of what to expect, isn't it?

If such is the case, why is it that in *Abbott and Costello Go to Mars* (1953) they don't ... they go to Venus? Or, if the title says *Abbott and Costello Meet the Killer, Boris Karloff* (1948), the often-evil Mr. K. is *not* the killer? Hmm.

In his delightful book, *Movie Clips* (Guinness Superlatives, 1989), Patrick Robertson also tells of the German film *Eine Nacht in London* (1934), which was released in Britain as *One Knight in London*. In the event that you're one of those who subscribe to Mark Twain's quote that "Life is too short to learn German," "Nacht" means "night." Dark knights are another matter entirely.

Robertson also tells us that the British *The Amorous Mr. Prawn* (1962) was about a general's wife who opens their official home to paying guests. However, in a display of unbelievable opportunism, the film was released in America as *The Playgirl and the War Minister*, notwithstanding that there was neither a playgirl nor a war minister in the film. It was, however, the year of the 1962 Profumo affair. Go figure.

Then, on the other hand, when the American Western *A Big Hand for the Little Lady* (1966) was released in Britain, it was retitled *Big Deal at Dodge City*, despite the fact that it took place not in Dodge City but in Laredo. (It was written initially for television as *Big Deal in Laredo*—at least *they* got it right.)

More titular tittering:

Did Anyone Tell Norman Schwarzkopf?

Adventures in Iraq (1943) took place in Syria. Does Saddam Hussein know about this?

An A.K.C. A.K.A.

Not only was there not a character named "Lassie" in *Courage of Lassie* (1946), but also the gender-crossing collie played Elizabeth Taylor's dog "Bill." In opera, they'd call it a "pants role." In film, it's just a way to get the star's name in the title.

ASPECTS OF THE BOOM TIMES

The most often noticed film flub is the appearance of a boom mike on screen. Perhaps more than any other glitch, a roving mike in the frame has the potential to grab your attention and distract you from the story or the onscreen action.

You should know that it's important to keep the boom mike as close as possible to the actors in order to get a good strong voice track—even though much of the track will be redone in the studio during a "looping" session—as well as to minimize outside noise. Essentially, two types of booms are used in films—a rolling boom, on which the mike is manipulated with pulleys and cables, and the more popular "fishpole" boom. The boom operator stands just outside the frame, holding the mike on a long fiberglass pole just over the actor's heads, moving it back and forth from speaker to speaker. The mike that some viewers see sneaking into the frame is usually a long tubular device, covered with either a foam or a shaggy fabric wind screen.

Oddly, one person may see a boom mike in a particular theater or in a television broadcast, while another may never see it—because it's not always there. This has to do with the many variations on the size and projection of the picture.

Since the beginning of the movie industry, there has been constant experimentation with screen size and masking, with camera and projector technology, and with projection booth automation. Add to this mix the possibility of human error (especially when today's projectionist might be a button-pushing high schooler in a computerized mall multiplex) and the chances of visible onscreen mishaps increase by quantum leaps.

The configuration of the picture you see on the screen is known as the *aspect ratio*. This is the relationship of the height of the screen to its width. Early filmmakers produced a picture that was relatively square, which evolved into what is now known as the "Academy Aperture." The width of the picture was about one third larger than the height, for a ratio of 1.33:1. It's still the shape of the frame on 35mm film. In the early 1950s, CinemaScope came along, with 2.35:1 ratio. Many theaters jumped onto the new standard—since all it involved was installation of a new screen and some new lenses for the projectors—as opposed to 3-D and Cinerama, which required a complete refitting. CinemaScope was shot on the same 35mm stock, but it was filmed through an anamorphic camera lens. This squeezed the picture onto the film and then, when shown through a similar anamorphic projection lens, it was spread back out on the screen. Since the CinemaScope patent was tightly held and distribution rigidly controlled, competitive systems quickly emerged—including some in which the top and bottom strips of the film frame were not used, with the middle, wide-shaped segment being magnified out to ratios such as 1.85:1, the size you see most often on today's screens. In some instances, the top and bottom strips were masked off; in others, the area was just not used for picture, giving ample room for boom mikes and all sorts of other things to roam around the top of the frame.

Another development was 70mm, which gave greater clarity on large screens for "road show" (reserved seats) engagements, and was then reduced to 35 mm CinemaScope for general release. It's still in use today, with some of the mega-pictures—such as Disney's recent restoration of *Fantasia* (1940) going out in both road show and wide-screen formats. One of the major advantages of 70mm is that it carries a magnetic sound track, vastly improving the sound quality. Also just emerging is digital sound, which takes film into the sound quality range of compact discs.

The number of film formats used over the years is awesome, and it's daunting to try and understand them. A few names: MetroScope, MegaScope, CinemaScope, VistaVision, WarnerScope, Camerascope, SuperScope, Tohoscope, Hammerscope, TechniScope, Franscope, Todd-AO, Camera 65, Cinerama 70, Vitascope, Vitarama, Super Technirama, Cinemiracle, and Panavision.

With all of the projection size possibilities, it's up to the local theater to properly mask its screen to give the image its best frame. If the masking is off or the projector framing slightly askew, there just might be some things at the top or bottom of the frame that the filmmakers didn't intend for you to see.

The better theaters have adjustable masking; they can move the black borders on the four sides of the screen to accommodate the proper aspect ratio of the particular film being shown. Others can move the side borders in and out, but the top and bottom bands are stationary. And still others—probably the majority—can't adjust their masking at all.

There are a few other elements to the aspect situation. One is the aperture plate in the projector. Quite frequently, unless the theater owner or projectionist cares enough (or knows enough) to change the aperture plate in the projector—the frame through which the film is projected—and adjust screen masking, a pre-1950s movie will be projected with the top and bottom lopped off. Heads and feet fall by the wayside, to say nothing of what happens to the director and cinematographer's careful compositions. You might even have the experience of seeing more than the director wanted to reveal to you—such as

John Denver's shorts, which show in an improper framing when he comes out of the shower in *Oh, God!* (1977).

Another cause of the microphone sneaking onto the screen is that often directors and script supervisors are watching the scene through a *video assist,* as it is being filmed. The camera operator is the only person who can see exactly what the lens is seeing, and he has to think about focus, lighting, all sorts of things. To enable others in the crew to see exactly what the camera's eye sees, either a small video camera is placed atop the film camera, or the film camera itself has a video tap, with a TV monitor elsewhere on the set. Quite often something out of the ordinary can be seen when it comes into the frame. But the picture is not as clear as that on your home TV set. Lighting on the set is designed for the film camera, not for the monitor, so things can slip right past, things like microphone intrusions.

Now, let's venture into another minefield. Until the home video explosion, movies were made to be shown in movie theaters, for better or worse. Television was at first no consideration, then only a minor one. Now it's a major consideration. Most movies will make a quick trip into the home video market, some within days of their theatrical release. (I recall commenting to a friend when we were leaving the press preview of the movie I consider the hands-down winner as the worst of 1990, *Fire Birds,* "This turkey will be in the video stores before we get home tonight!")

At any rate, when a wide-screen movie is converted for television or home video use, there's no way the entire image can be seen on a television screen—unless the picture is "letterboxed," the method preferred by most film buffs as well as by the directors and cinematographers who worked so hard to create a specific onscreen experience. But the letterbox, with its black bands at the top and bottom of the TV picture, creates a relatively small image on the screen. This naturally takes away some of the intimacy of the image unless you have a mega-monitor or projection TV.

So most films are "panned and scanned." (The pan, incidentally, has nothing to do with the way it was reviewed by the critics!) A video operator scans the film, panning back and forth across the wide image to record the relatively square portion of the picture that will appear on your TV when you run the videocassette. Rarely are the craftsmen who made the film involved with it in the studio during this process, and the meticulously-composed work of a world-class director or cinematographer is left to the judgment of a video technician.

"Pan and scan" produces some Hollywood horror stories—leaving an actor in what was originally a two-shot talking to thin air, or, as in one of the Fred Astaire-Ginger Rogers movies where Ginger dances right off the screen and back on again. That certainly wasn't in the director's plan.

The next time you see a "letterboxed" movie on TV or videocassette, imagine what you'd be seeing if you had to select only about two-thirds of the picture. That's what happens when it's panned and scanned. And that's what happened particularly to Gene Kelly and Stanley Donen's wonderful 1955 *It's Always Fair Weather,* when Kelly's meticulously choreographed "Ash Can Dance" featuring Michael Kidd, Dan Dailey and

himself performing in three side-by-side screen panels was completely destroyed when only two-thirds of the scene could be accommodated in the panned and scanned version for TV.

When the film is converted to TV, there's a good chance that the errant mike boom and other glitches and gaffes that were seen on the theater screen are caught by the video operator and cut out of the picture—or, due to the exigencies of the "home cutoff" on various TV sets (the picture you see at home is about a half-inch smaller all the way around than the one on TV studio monitors), may or may not be in the home video or broadcast versions. The lesson is that while boom intrusions are the most frequent of film flubs, the mike you see may not be seen by someone else, unless of course it's way into the frame.

A recent example of a flub being lost to "pan and scan" is in *The Two Jakes* (1990). When Jack Nicholson is going into a beauty salon in a scene set in the late 1940s, in the theatrical version of the film a Bank of America automatic teller machine can be seen in the background—something that didn't exist at the time of the film. But in the home video version, there's just a hint of the machine at the right side of the frame.

The purpose of this little dissertation is not so much to reveal the mike boom film flubs (don't leave—they're coming), but to give me the opportunity to preach my particular sermon—that most movies should be seen in theaters.

Shortly after *FILM FLUBS* was published, I took some heat from home video magazines and video rental stores about my statement that "the only real way to see a movie remains on a big screen in a real movie theater." Even though I'm as good a customer as the video business will ever have, I stand by my guns.

With the exception of made-for-television films and some low-budget turkeys, movies are made to be seen on the big screen. Not only do you get the best visual presentation (hopefully), but you become part of the shared audience experience.

I know many film critics who prefer to do their viewing in an audience setting, rather than by themselves in a screening room. The effect of shared laughter and tears, suspense and terror, beauty and excitement, is very much a part of the moviegoing experience. Movies are made to be seen by audiences, and seeing a movie in a crowded theater on a big screen can only heighten the experience.

Besides, who can really enjoy a movie without fresh popcorn? Microwave popcorn, as much as I love it, isn't worth the butter it's cooked in.

Just hope that you can find one of the few theaters where the operators really *care* about films and their exhibition, where the floors aren't sticky or smelly, and the seats comfortable. Sadly, it's becoming a quixotic quest.

At the risk of treading on some toes of very good friends in the movie business, I have to say this: When you want to see a really important film or one that has some special meaning for you, seek out the biggest and best theater that you can find, preferably a single-screen house. If you are lucky enough to have nearby an old movie palace, restored or otherwise, that's not playing action/adventure trash movies, go see it there. Go, even if, as in Los Angeles and many other major cities, the film you want to see is running with foreign-language subtitles. You might learn a new language!

One of my close friends produced the landmark *Altered States* (1980). I first saw it in a movie house with the sound system set up to the producer and director's specifications. Later, I saw it on cable television and home video. It's virtually two different movies.

We were discussing the film recently, and agreed that the film loses about two-thirds of its power on television. In the movie theater, with its big screen and powerful sound system, *Altered States* will literally peel your skin off. Roger Ebert said in his review, "I can tell myself that this movie is a fiendishly constructed visual and verbal roller coaster, a movie deliberately intended to overwhelm its audiences with sensual excess. I know all that, and yet I *was* overwhelmed, I *was* caught up in its headlong energy." He's absolutely right, and the film itself is one of the best demonstrations of the reason movies should first be seen on the big screen.

An Ivy League college student son of some friends told me he had been going to movies all of his life, but he'd never seen one in any theater other than a shopping-mall multiplex. After having viewed *Gone With the Wind* several times on television and once at a multiplex, the night before our conversation he had seen the restored *GWTW* print perfectly projected at a special screening in a magnificently-restored large-screen movie palace. He was absolutely dazzled by the experience. Not only did the film itself take on an entirely new meaning and depth, but he had no idea that a movie could look like that and could have such an emotional impact. It was, he said, an experience he would never forget.

But home video is wonderful, too. It's a great medium for seeing a film when you can't afford to go to the theater, especially with the outrageous prices that are being charged at the box office these days. It's wonderful for keeping movies alive, for exposing new generations to the great films of cinematic history; for allowing you to savor a favorite movie or favorite actor's performance time and again; for studying the techniques of great directors, writers, cinematographers, and other crafts people; for a terrific evening at home with friends, and as an alternative to TV's mind-numbing sitcommery. And home video, being relatively immune to the box-office numbers, is often the only way to see wonderful little movies that slip on and off the screens when they can't cut it in the mass market, and to see foreign films as well.

End of sermon. Pass the offering plate. Let's now get down to business. And don't blame me if you don't see these mistakes—they may be lost in the translation from film to TV, even from one TV set to another.

Boom Times

When Anjelica Huston and John Cusack are talking in the living room of his apartment in *The Grifters* (1990), the mike boom dips into the scene. The shadow of the mike also falls across Scarlett O'Hara's dress in a scene from *Gone With the Wind* (1939).

One reader reported that when he saw *Friday the 13th, Part VI: Jason Lives* (1986), the boom mike came into the picture so often that people in the theater were booing it.

The boom mike can be seen reflected in the shiny top of a jukebox when John Travolta and Olivia Newton-John meet at the malt shop in *Grease* (1978). And it cruises across the top of the screen as Warren Beatty comes down a staircase in *Heaven Can Wait* (1978).

In the classic *North by Northwest* (1959), watch for the microphone looming over Cary Grant and Eva Marie Saint during a conversation in the Chicago train station. It also makes frequent appearances in *Executive Action* (1973), especially in the scenes with Will Geer.

A microphone comes into frame in the wedding scene in *The Ruling Class* (1972) and literally hangs around for the rest of the ceremony. And a dramatic shot in *The Trip to Bountiful*, (1985), when Geraldine Page is standing in the middle of a cornfield, is spoiled when the microphone pops into view.

A variation on the meandering mike theme occurs in *The Big Chill* (1983) when Kevin Kline is wearing a body microphone, which you can see when his sweatshirt clings to his body. He should be glad that he didn't share the experience of Leslie Nielsen, who wears his RF mike to the john in *Naked Gun* (1988), or that of the actor, who shall go nameless (because the sound man wouldn't tell us), who forgot that he was wearing a live, switched-on RF mike when he went back to the trailer for a "quickie" during a break. The crew was, of course, gloriously entertained.

Three Men and a Baby (The Ghost Story)

It's one of the best things that ever happened to video rentals. Somebody started one of those strange rumors about the appearance of a ghost in *Three Men and a Baby* (1987) and word spread. All over America people were rushing to rent or buy the video so they could see the ghost. Let's have a little talk about it.

Here's what you'll see: When Olympia Dukakis goes toward the baby's crib, she passes a floor-to-ceiling window in which you see nothing. She picks up the baby and walks back past the window as she talks to Ted Danson. This time there's what appears to be a little boy peeking in on the scene.

A rumor got started that this was the ghost of a little boy who had died in the house where the movie was said to be filmed. It became one of those stories that everyone wanted to believe. The Disney switchboard was inundated. I talked to the person who had to take most of the calls, and she said she was nearly driven nuts. People didn't believe the official explanation. They wanted to believe what they wanted to believe.

She's the same person, incidentally, who had to take the calls when someone thought they saw an erect penis drawn into the towers of the castle on the poster and cassette cover of *The Little Mermaid*. She said that there were days when she felt like answering the phone "Penis Central." And, in case you're wondering, it sorta looks like that's what it is, but I'm sure it's accidental. (No commercial artist who ever wants to work again would try to pull off a trick like that.)

Anyway, back to the topic. Touchstone (the Disney division that produced the picture) maintains, as the official company explanation, that what you see in *Three Men and a Baby* is a portion of a cardboard cutout of Ted Danson wearing a fez, a prop that would tie in with his role as a flamboyant commercial actor/model. Touchstone says it was put into place accidentally. That's the party line.

The entire situation is ripe with fallacies. In the first place, even if you do believe in ghosts, you have to accept that tenet that they can't be photographed. There's nothing there of the kind of substance that would reflect light into a camera.

Second, even though the "ghost" story makes a good one, the scene was *not* shot in an apartment in New York where a small child had died. It was shot on a soundstage in Toronto. It was a movie set, and no one had ever died on that stage.

Third, it's too hard to keep secrets on a set. There are just too many people involved. If that had been a ghost, if it had been verifiable as a ghost, if there was any substance to the story (or the image) at all, it doubtless would have been front-page news in every paper in the country. Trust me. And if you don't trust me, remember that Leonard Nimoy directed the movie. He would have told us. Vulcans can't lie.

I'll have to say that Der Flubmeister here doesn't buy the entire Touchstone line on the incident. I've looked at the tape several times, and I feel that it really is a little boy. A real, live, flesh and blood child who happened to be on the set and peeked in through the window, getting caught by the camera. The "cutout" story seems fairly fallacious to me.

At any rate, whatever it is, it is indeed a film flub. It's something that shouldn't have been on the film, shouldn't have been seen, shouldn't have broken the story line. And I'll believe it's a ghost the same day that I have proof that a UFO lands at Harvard and the denizens chat with an astronomy prof, instead of landing in a swamp and kidnapping a hillbilly.

(For a similar tale, consider the *Wizard of Oz* "suicide" on page 43).

MEET THE CREW

Hard as they try to stay behind the camera, members of the film crew might be quickly glimpsed if you really keep a keen eye on the screen. There's a lot going on on a set, much for everyone to do even when the camera is running, and at times it's difficult to keep out of the eye of the lens.

I recall being on a set where a nine-camera night shot was underway. In order to get that many angles, it was impossible to keep all of the cameras out of each other's sight. So the designers put bushes, rocks, even a car in front of some of the cameras so they couldn't be seen by each other. On signal, all of the camera operators had to hide behind their camouflage. It worked: Not only did the complicated shot—involving rain effects, a helicopter, and a car explosion—come off without a hitch, but it was pulled off in only one take. The crew, expecting to spend the night on the set, actually got to go home early. But it doesn't always happen that way.

The problem is compounded by the penchant of many directors to keep the camera constantly on the move. Hitchcock was famous for it, and Brian DePalma carries on in his tradition, as do many other contemporary directors. In fact, these days it's fairly common for the camera grips to lay rails to take the camera through long tracking shots or to build special rigs to keep the actors and the camera on the same

plane. Notice that the rails actually, if inadvertently, made it on screen in *Pee-wee's Big Adventure* (1985) as Pee-wee passes a series of offbeat signs.

Reflections are a real bugaboo. After all, a window pane, a shiny surface, a mirror is going to reflect exactly what it sees. Hopefully, the cinematographers have avoided the problem with their camera placements. Dulling sprays, masking, even placing cameras at oblique angles are among the techniques used to keep the equipment out of the shot. But when there's just a moment of inattention ...

Everything That Goes Around ...

Shortly after a big musical number in *Beaches* (1988), Bette Midler and Barbara Hershey go into an apartment building through revolving doors. As the door spins around, look for the camera crew in a shiny reflection.

Walk on By

Director Harry Beaumont must have let things get a little sloppy on the set of *The Floradora Girl* (1930), starring Marion Davies. At one point, a crew member walks right in front of the camera; on another, you can see the clapboard. Or was Davies's sugar daddy William Randolph Hearst hanging around the set and making Beaumont nervous?

He Didn't Get Out Fast Enough

During a struggle in Charlie Sheen's room in *The Rookie* (1989) between his wife and the bad guys, as they spin around the room the camera catches a brief glimpse of one of the crew.

The musical *Seven Brides for Seven Brothers* (1954) features several lavish Michael Kidd numbers, including one where the brothers are dancing outside their rustic house. On the right in the background, you can see the knees and feet of several stagehands working above the set.

Sneaking a Peak

We couldn't expect you to be overly attentive to detail during a scene in Brian DePalma's *Body Double* (1984) when a porn movie is being filmed. But check out the mirror on the door in Melanie Griffith's room for a brief glimpse of the camera crew. On the other hand, give DePalma and cinematographer Stephen H. Burum credit for being able to pull off a scene that was fraught with opportunities for error in a scene when the camera takes a 360° spin. In that instance, a special rig was built to carry the camera crew and the actors for the merry-go-round effect.

We're Just Looking for a Book

Michael Douglas is in the library in *Fatal Attraction* (1987) talking with Stuart Pankin about the affair with Glenn Close when an employee pushes a cart of books past a French door—with the camera crew mirrored in it.

The Wizard of Oz

We're off to see the Wizard. As we go down the Yellow Brick Road, it's time to look for some film flubs and other glitches in a movie that's probably been seen by more people on the planet Earth than anything Hollywood has ever produced. As such, it opens the door to many a flub-spotting expedition, with so many folks looking at it so closely. But the interesting thing is that you're so charmed by the story that the flubs can just slip on by. But we'd better get started, before the Wicked Witch finds us.

In *FILM FLUBS,* there was discussion at length about Dorothy's hair length, the Cowardly Lion's crown, and the Tin Man's faulty brain. This time, we're going to head further down the Yellow Brick Road to tell you about some more Oz flubbery.

In the early sepia-toned scenes, Auntie Em is taking some chickens out of the incubator. She counts "sixty-seven, sixty-eight, sixty-nine." She then puts three more in her apron and takes one from Dorothy, counting, "seventy." It should have been seventy-three.

Dorothy has one heck of a dry cleaner. First, when she falls into the pigpen, she doesn't get dirty. Later, she has two spots on her dress when she's on the dirt road talking to Toto, but in the next scene, she's clean.

An oil lamp that was on the table by the window earlier has disappeared before the window is blown open by the storm; and when her bed is sliding all over the room during the tornado and pictures are moving about on the walls, notice that bottles on the table don't even move.

There's an interesting situation with the background footage during the tornado scene. The background that you see when Auntie Em and the farmhands go into the storm cellar is different from that when Dorothy tries to enter it a few moments later. It appears to be the footage we saw when Dorothy comes into the house through the front door.

There's another interesting switcheroo when Dorothy is watching the action outside the window as the house flies through the air. It's clear that there is a curtained window behind her, yet when the house lands, the window's gone, replaced by a wall with a bundt cake pan hanging on.

Throughout the film, Dorothy can't seem to hang on to sweets. Early on, the cruller she's eating disappears before she sings "Over the Rainbow." Then we never discover what happens to the lollipop (brought on by our buddy Jerry Maren) and flowers that she had in her hand after Glenda the Good Witch leaves.

All sorts of things go awry when Dorothy and friends are in the Witch's Castle. In the first place, notice that the sign pointing the way is misspelled. It says "Witches Castle."

Next, the Tin Man chops down the door with an ax he didn't have as he climbed the stairs. And, as Dorothy and pals run down the stairs, they start out as Scarecrow, Dorothy, Tin Woodsman, and the Lion. There is a quick cut to the cackling witch, then the order is Scarecrow, Tin Woodsman, Dorothy, and the Lion.

Another point to ponder is that it's always the brainless Scarecrow who seems to come up with the ideas that get them out of a jam.

Before the Wicked Witch of the West sends her flying monkeys to capture Dorothy and friends in the Haunted Forest, a line of dialogue was mistakenly left in. She tells the head monkey that she has "sent a little insect on ahead to take the fight out of them." This refers to a song-and-dance sequence featuring "The Jitterbug," a little insect that causes its victims to dance wildly until they are exhausted. The sequence was cut from the film after preview showings—but you can see it on the laserdisc version of the movie.

Just before meeting the Cowardly Lion, Dorothy, the Tin Man, and the Scarecrow head down the road, singing "We're Off to See the Wizard." Something is going on in the background that has engendered one of those strange film legends. Indeed you can see a figure moving about among the scenery trees just beyond the little house that sits beside the road. It appears to be a crew member who was caught on the set when the camera was running. The word that was circulating among those who choose to believe it was that a crew member had actually committed suicide on the set, hanging himself from the tree.

C'mon, now. Do you think if that was indeed the case, Hollywood could have kept it quiet all these years? This is a town where everything is public knowledge. Everything. It's a town where an out-of-work actress named Peg Entwhistle became the stuff of legend when she committed suicide by jumping off the "H" of the HOLLYWOOD sign. Where Jon Erik Hexum made worldwide headlines when he accidentally killed himself on the set of his TV show. Where every sordid moment of filmdom's past has been exposed by books such as Kenneth Anger's *Hollywood Babylon,* by the Grave Line Tours, and God knows whatall else.

We even went so far as to check with a leading authority on the movie, Aljean Harmetz, the respected *New York Times* reporter who wrote the book, *The Making of "The Wizard of Oz."* She said that if it had ever happened, it was news to her.

Granted, there were some serious production problems on the set. The Wicked Witch (Margaret Hamilton) was so badly burned in a special effects accident that she had to be hospitalized, and Buddy Ebsen, originally cast to play the Tin Woodsman, nearly died from the effects of the silver makeup.

But this one, we believe, falls into the realm of things that would certainly be interesting if they really had happened. Things like the ghost of a little boy in *Three Men and a Baby* (see page 30). Like Procter & Gamble promoting satanism through their corporate logo. Like the story of the gift-wrapped dead cat. Like the alligator in the toilet. We await refutation.

COSTUME CHANGES

It's tough enough to find (or make) clothing and footwear to fit a certain period, but when the costume supervisor has to be sure that the actor is wearing thc same outfit from shot to shot, there's plenty of opportunity for the gaffe gremlins to sneak into the scene. Sometimes, there's good reason for the costume change when, for example, an actor trades cowboy boots for sneakers to make a difficult jump. But you'd think there would be ways around that—like building boot tops onto sneakers, keeping the feet out of the shot, or whatever.

Or perhaps they hope you just won't notice. But in these days of freeze-frame and slo-mo on VCR's and laser disc players, they don't have a chance. Someone will discover the subtle difference.

Take, for example, the stunt woman who doubled for Joanna Cassidy (Zhora) in *Blade Runner* (1982). There's an exciting chase scene when she jumps through a plate glass window wearing a bikini go-go costume covered with a clear plastic outer garment. Word was that when the stunt woman first performed the scene, she was actually cut by the breaking candy glass. So the scene was reshot and the stunt double wears a protective body suit under the plastic outfit. Look closely as she comes through the window and you'll see the sleeve of the protective suit, even though in most other shots she's bare-armed and wearing little more than the bikini under the plastic. Actresses should be careful about wearing clear plastic. Was this a precursor of Laura (*Twin Peaks*) Palmer's fate?

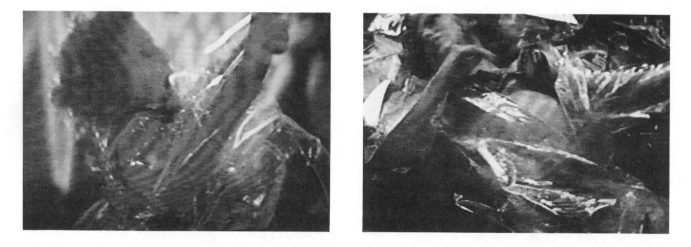

There are other problems that pop up from shot to shot especially when the shot-to-shot sequence is on the set itself, day to day. Things change. They really do.

Shot to Shot, Shoe to Shoe

At the ending of *Above the Law* (1988), Steven Seagal is fighting a group of terrorists in a grocery store. As the police cars approach, he grabs one of the thugs and uses him as a shield to crash through the store's front window. He leaps forward wearing black leather boots but lands on the sidewalk in Reebok tennis shoes.

Sneakering Through the Window

Similarly, in *The First Power* (1990), Lou Diamond Phillips wears silver-tipped cowboy boots throughout most of the movie. When he climbs through a church window he's wearing sneakers which then become cowboy boots again when he jumps out the window and runs down the street.

She Wasn't in Much of a Hurry

Vicki Vale (Kim Basinger) is told about the Wayne family tragedy in *Batman* (1989). She rushes to see Bruce Wayne, but somewhere along the way she must have stopped off to spruce up, because she arrives in a different dress and hairstyle.

The $330 Loss

Kim Basinger wants to purchase a $300 scarf at a flea market in *9½ Weeks* (1986). But she takes a wiser course and buys instead a $30 set of ducks, which she puts into a shopping bag. Mickey Rourke then surprises her with the scarf and drapes it over her shoulders. They walk to the waterfront, but by the time they get there, she's neither wearing the scarf nor carrying the shopping bag.

Tied to Be Fit

Sam Waterston can't keep up with his tie in a scene from Woody Allen's *September* (1987). The movie has much to do with the expression of angst during a weekend in Vermont (has there ever been a Woody Allen movie *sans* angst?). Waterston's is so severe that during a conversation with Jack Warden, his necktie is alternately tied and untied at regular intervals.

I'm So Blue, Part Two

Judy Garland dances with little sister Margaret O'Brien in *Meet Me in St. Louis* (1944). Margaret starts out in pink house slippers, but later in the dance she generously lifts her nightie to show us that they've turned blue.

Awakenings

We hope the Marshall family won't be upset with us. We've said much about Garry Marshall's *Pretty Woman* (1990), now we're starting in on sister Penny Marshall's *Awakenings* (1990). But, like most Hollywood professionals, they're gracious about the flubs spotted in their films. Penny, in fact, even told an interviewer about a couple to look for. But we love you, Marshalls. We really do.

But let us marshall our resources (sorry about that!). In *Awakenings*, when Dr. Sayer (Robin Williams) is testing the "frozen" Lucy (Alice Drummond) for her reflexes, notice the changing position of her eyes from shot to shot.

When the patients are listening to an opera recording, Dr. Sayer and nurse Eleanor Costello (Julie Kavner) watch them for reactions. The over-the-shoulder shot behind the three patients at the table shows quite a wind outside the open window, blowing the patients' hair. Yet when the camera does a full close-up on the woman in the middle, her hair is perfectly still.

In the scene where the awakened Leonard (Robert De-Niro) is working on an architectural model with his mother (Ruth Nelson) seated next to him, he leaves to follow Paula (Penelope Ann Miller). When he looks back at his mother, there's a full paper bag on the seat which he just vacated.

A telephone company executive took note of the modular handset on Dr. Sayer's telephone. The film was set in 1969, when hard-wired connections were used. The modular connections came along in the mid-1970s.

And finally, the Marshalls do have problems with buttons (see *Pretty Woman,* page 7). Near the close of the film, Dr. Sayer runs downstairs to meet Eleanor. His coat is buttoned in the long shots and open in the closeups.

JEWELRY THEFTS AND OTHER PROP PROBLEMS

The disappearance of jewelry seems to lead the parade of cinematic prop problems. For some reason, it's a constant source of glitches, gaffes, and goofs. One can assume that it must have to do with the fact that the actors tend to remove the prop jewelry if there's a long wait between takes—or if the same costume is worn over several days' shooting, the costume supervisor just forgets to put the jewelry back on before the cameras roll for the day.

But there are other prop glitches—the most noticeable usually being misspellings or the use of things that shouldn't oughta be there. Into the jewelry box and prop closet we go:

Henry Didn't Raise No Fool

Peter Fonda proves that dad Henry didn't raise a fool, in the opening of *Easy Rider* (1969). After scoring on a drug deal, Peter and Dennis Hopper get ready to start out on their motorcycles for New Orleans and Mardi Gras. Fonda is seen stuffing his share of the money into a plastic tube, which he slips into the gas tank of his bike. Notice that he's wearing an expensive Rolex watch when he screws down the cap. In the next scene, he and Hopper pause in the desert while he symbolically strips off

the watch and throws it away. This time it's a cheap Timex, with a Twist-O-Flex band. There's even a close-up of the cheap watch ticking away on the ground.

The Spare Box

Alan Ladd, while seated on a high porch in *Whispering Smith* (1949), takes a harmonica out of his inside coat pocket, throws away the box, then plays a tune. When he's finished, he reaches back into his pocket, takes out another box, and puts the harmonica into it.

Misplaced Maple Leafs

Canadians noticed that the liquor crates in a warehouse raid in *The Untouchables* (1987), set in the 1930s, were printed with the stylized maple leaf symbol. However, the maple leaf didn't come into use as a logo in Canada until 1965, when the Maple Leaf flag was unfurled. In other films, Canadians laugh when they see the Royal Mounted Police on horseback. Despite the name, the Mounties appear on horseback only on ceremonial occasions. It's been years since they patrolled in the saddle.

Midair Collusions

Tom Cruise's wristwatch changes during the training flight in *Top Gun* (1986) from the one he had on when he boarded the plane. But then again, what can we expect since in the final battle the tail number on his plane changes several times in mid-flight?

Postdate the Check

The date on the payoff check in *The Verdict* (1982) isn't consistent with the rest of the dates in the film, which are shown on phone bills and the like. Producer David Brown told Wayne Norman of radio station WILI-AM in Willimantic, Conn., that the date may well have been the day that the scene was shot.

D'Artagnan Dunnit

Milady DeWinter (Lana Turner) is lavishly bejewelled in *The Three Musketeers* (1948), except for a brief moment when the baubles disappear before our eyes.

Physician, Heal Thyself

When Chevy Chase is impersonating a doctor in *Fletch* (1985), in the front shots he has a stethoscope in his ears, but from the back it's hanging around his neck. Similarly, in *Tie Me Up, Tie Me Down* (1990), the cord from the doctor's glasses catches on her ear, pops off, then back on again. In the same film, notice that Marina, the porn star, wears no panties when she dons a short dress, but when she takes it off, panties have magically appeared.

A Film Noir Gets Noirer

We have some serious questions about things that went on in *The Grifters* (1990), Stephen Frears's riveting *film noir*. In the first place, when Annette Bening is being very sexy and leans over John Cusack, she pulls off her large gold earrings. What happened to them? When they leave the room, neither she nor John are wearing them.

Then another time, Annette comes into John's room in a slinky black dress for a chat, but as she leaves she has somehow picked up a shoulder strap purse. Why was it in his room? Was it his?

We have to wonder also if there was an intermediary stop to shop in *The Grifters* when mean old Pat Hingle takes Anjelica Huston away. She gets into his car wearing a plain white shift, and gets out with a belt added. Did they stop and buy it, or was it stashed in her purse?

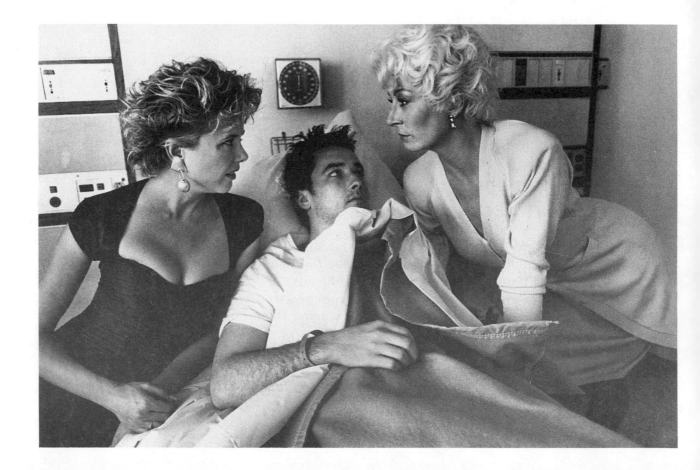

Dances With Wolves

Dances With Wolves (1990) is a fine, fine movie. That's why it troubles us so much to have to point out a few of its flubs. But we have our work to do, and we continue undaunted.

Perhaps the most notable of its glitches happens when the wagon driver Timmons (Robert Pastorelli) takes John Dunbar (Kevin Costner) to the cavalry outpost. It's one of those instances where the old saying about getting egg on one's face becomes cinematic reality. The driver takes a bite of a pickled egg, then when Costner tells him to leave him at the abandoned fort, he spews it out, getting some on his mustache. Then he looks over to Costner, and the egg is gone. In the next shot, it's back again.

And speaking of Timmons, one person who saw the movie wondered why the Indians could down a bison with a single arrow, but it took four to kill Timmons. And even after he's dead and scalped, he appears to take a breath.

We wondered about Mary McDonnell's hair. In the first

place, it changes length in the scene when Dunbar first finds her mourning the death of her husband. But even more important, if, as the story says, she has lived with the Indians since she was a child, how come she's the only one with a shag hairdo? Why isn't her hair styled like the rest of the Indian women?

Another alert flub spotter noticed that when the soldiers are cleaning their rifles, one is wearing a wedding ring—a tradition that didn't come along until much later. There was also much discussion of Costner's use of the rather modern expression, "Hi!"

We leave with a couple of notes from experts in their field, who also found minute details which caught their eye. One hunter noticed a feather from a ring-necked pheasant in an Indian's headdress, saying that the bird wouldn't have been in that part of the country during the era of the movie. Another noticed that when the flock of birds flies overhead, the sound effect is that of Canadian Honkers, but the birds are actually Sandhill Cranes. And an apple grower reported that a partly-eaten Red Delicious apple is seen in the Civil War scene. The Red Delicious is a treat that didn't appear until around 1900. And, hey, how come the dead wolf seems to be wearing a choke chain collar? Our flub spotters know their stuff.

ILL LOGIC

The most delightful film flubs are the ones that provoke the "huh?" reaction—those that make you scratch your head and wonder what was going on when the picture was being prepared.

As we tiptoe onto some dangerous ground, let's think for a moment about the pivotal problem in one of the all-time great movies—*Citizen Kane* (1941). The entire film is devoted to finding the meaning of Charles

Foster Kane's (Orson Welles) dying word: "Rosebud." Yet it seems that there is no one in the room to hear the faintly-whispered word. Later in the film, Kane's butler, Paul Stewart, says something that implies that he was there. If he was, he must have been way off in a corner and had wonderfully keen hearing.

A prime example of the "huh?" reaction can be found in *Die Hard 2* (1990) when the film tries harder to supply us with a series of logic errors. The first of these errors provides what has to be our favorite contemporary film flub. Hundreds of dedicated flub-spotters and even casual movie fans will notice that when Bruce Willis makes a call in Dulles Airport in Washington, D. C., he does it from a pay telephone that

clearly says "Pacific Bell." We'll have to give director Renny Harlin and his coworkers a bit of sympathy, since they not only had to chase all over the country to find an airport that would accommodate a film which paints such an ugly picture of airports, but also had to chase snow all over the country. So confused were the filmmakers that they let Bruce call up his wife who is in the airplane. That's not much of a feat until you consider that airphones work from the plane to the ground, not from the ground to the plane.

But there's more. Before the terrorists seize Dulles Airport, head controller Trudeau (Fred Dalton Thompson—the lawyer-turned-actor who seemingly pops up on the screen as often as Michael Caine!) tells his staff that the Nashville Airport has shut down due to a severe snowstorm. But later, Dulles controllers, after little more than an hour, divert airplanes to alternate cities including Atlanta and Nashville. Yep, Nashville, with its closed-down, snowed-in runways.

More head-scratchers:

Selective Reflections

It's a given in ghost lore that ghosts don't cast reflections. But in one scene in *Beetlejuice* (1988), even though you can't see the reflections of the ghosts (Geena Davis and Alec Baldwin) in the mirror, you can certainly see them reflected in a windowpane.

Is a Bird Bath the Fountain of Youth?

The story of *Birdy* (1984) is told in flashbacks which alternate between two G.I.'s (Matthew Modine and Nicolas Cage) who are in their early twenties in 1972 but are sixteen-year-olds in the 1950s—indicating that they have aged only about four or five years over a course of seventeen or eighteen. What are they eating?

A Cop Car the Crooks Would Love

In *Another 48 HRS* (1990), Eddie Murphy and Nick Nolte sit in the back of a police car talking to a man. They finish the conversation and then open the rear doors to get out. Think about it. A police car, with rear doors that open from the inside. The bad guys love it.

Selective Grunge

Jack Nickolson's face is eaten by a grungy substance in *Batman* (1989). But it doesn't bother his deck of cards—paper being tougher than skin, we suppose.

Close Encounters With the Postal Service

Richard Dreyfuss is throwing dirt out the window in the original version of *Close Encounters of the Third Kind* (1977), while an extra, dressed as a mailman, looks on with amazement. A real-life neighbor who lived across the street in Mobile, Alabama, when the movie was filmed, told us that he himself was amazed by the mailman, since, as you can see, the neighborhood has mailboxes by the curb, which are filled not by a walking mailman but from a mail truck. Incidentally, the scene seems to have been cut in the Special Edition video.

Wendy and the Wind

It's a stormy night in Scotland when Wendy Hiller, a headstrong young lady on her way to marry a very rich man, is forced to stay over in a coastal house in *I Know Where I'm Going* (1945). The storm makes passage to the island impossible. She paces around the room while it rages outside. Inside the curtains blow even though the windows are closed. What a drafty house!

Sure ... You Try It

Knowledgeable audiences laughed in *No Way Out* (1987) when a character says that it will take twenty-four hours to check every corridor in the Pentagon. It would take days, maybe. Probably weeks.

A Look at the Books

When an alert movie buff saw Thomas More examining some ancient tomes in *A Man for All Seasons* (1966), she wondered why the books that characters pick up in historical movies are musty, dusty, and often ragged? It happens again in *Anne of the Thousand Days* (1969). If the films are true to the times, wouldn't most of the books be new? (And by the way: did anyone in Columbia's advertising department notice that Orson Welles's name was misspelled in the stills from the movie?)

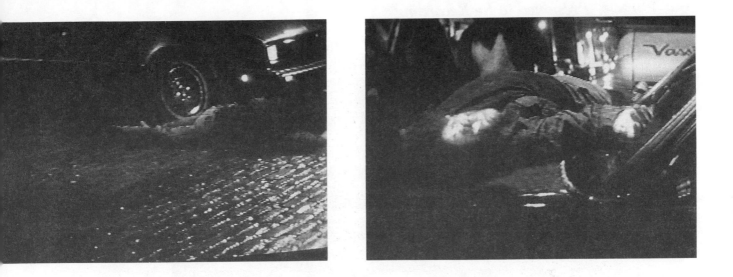

The Moving Dead

When Rick Aviles, playing a bad guy in *Ghost* (1990), is hit by a car and killed, notice that his dead body is lying on the street next to the car wheel as his spirit emerges. But when the spirit takes a disbelieving look at his corpse, it has moved upward and is on the hood.

Presumed to Be Recording

Having once interviewed two of Hollywood's top producers with dead batteries in my tape recorder, your humble scribe can certainly sympathize with the reporter who thrusts a tape recorder in Harrison Ford's face as he leaves the courthouse in *Presumed Innocent* (1990). You can see that there's no cassette in it; the recorder is empty.

Another Angle on Eastwood

In the scene about Clint Eastwood's "rape" in *The Rookie* (1990), a video was shot with the camera facing Eastwood. There is only one camera and it's turned on and left running. Thus all the shots should be from the same angle. But when the video is played back it's from several different angles.

Love Means Never Having to Say It Makes Sense

Love Story (1970) is a relatively simplistic tale, offering little to think about. But consider this: Jenny (Ali MacGraw) and Oliver (Ryan O'Neal) are at a skating rink when she tells him she's ready to go to the hospital. They trudge up a snowy hill and at the top they hail a cab for the trip. Later, after Jenny dies, Oliver walks out of the hospital, crosses the street, and walks down the hill to the same skating rink. If the hospital was right across the street, why did they take a cab earlier?

Sorry, Wrong Number

Tony Randall phones Doris Day from Rock Hudson's telephone in *Pillow Talk* (1959), getting a busy signal. But the plot line of the movie is based on the fact that Rock and Doris are on a party line. And in the 1989 TV remake of *Sorry, Wrong Number* with Loni Anderson, why does her husband call her person-to-person from a phone booth (to establish an alibi) when he knows she's bedridden and alone in their house?

Misery

If you want to learn just about everything you need to know about acting, watch Kathy Bates's bravura, Oscar-winning performance in *Misery* (1990). Her portrait of the mood swings and madness of an obsessed fan jumps right from the screen and rivets you to your seat. You'll leave the theater absolutely stunned.

But if you have just a moment to direct your attention elsewhere, take a look at the "sticky notes" on the sheriff's bulletin board. They move around all over the place, from shot to shot. Likewise, notice that when the sheriff and his wife are coming down the mountain, the road is covered with snow. But when he spots something and goes to investigate, Bates drives by on a road where the snow is melted away.

One person noticed that even though James Caan's car is referred to as a 1965 Mustang, it's actually a 1966 model. Sharp eyes.

There's also a glitch during one of the instances when Bates leaves Caan alone in the house. She drives away, but a shot shows that her car's in the driveway after she's gone; it's not there when she's back.

The typewriter which Caan acquires from his "number one fan" is missing an "n," but it seems to be just fine in a close-up.

Also, when Caan burns his manuscript and the curtain catches fire, he douses the flame. When the camera pans up, though, it appears that the flame has jumped to the top of the curtain, but no one puts it out.

Finally, there appears to be some ambiguity about the rip in the mattress where Caan stores his medicine. In several of the shots, it looks to be tightly sewn together.

NUMBERS GAME

Most of the time, when there's a juicy little film flub, it's not too difficult to ferret out the cause—whether a mistake on the part of someone in the crew, an oversight, something that wasn't researched carefully enough, or a moment of inattention. Then again, some flubs really don't have any logical explanation.

Six Plus Six Equals Seventeen

When Sundance (Robert Redford) reloads his two six-shooters in a gun battle in *Butch Cassidy and the Sundance Kid* (1969), he then gets off at least seventeen shots.

They'll Never Find Him Now

In an episode of TV's *Quantum Leap*, Sam Beckett (Scott Bakula) is living in the Watts area of Los Angeles during the 1960s riots. He asks Al (Dean Stockwell) where his (Sam's) apartment is. Al tells him that it's 218, but in the next scene, when Sam is in the apartment and the outside door is opened, it's 217.

A Baker's Dozen of Miscounts

There are only ten women in *Thirteen Women* (1932), a movie about a girl (Myrna Loy) of mixed racial heritage out to avenge childhood mistreatment by murdering her tormentors. But, just to make up for the slight, *Her Twelve Men* (1954) has Greer Garson teaching a private-school class of thirteen boys.

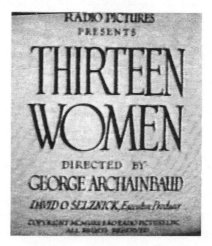

One More Time

A bad guy with a six-shooter takes aim at Tommy Lee Jones in *Black Moon Rising* (1986) ... and fires seven shots.

Increasing the Odds

If George Bush couldn't remember "the date that will live in infamy," should we fault Otto Preminger for recreating the Battle of Pearl Harbor for *In Harm's Way* (1965) with nine U.S. Navy battleships, one more than was actually there on December 7, 1941?

Where Are the Other Two?

King Kong (1933) has the great ape in chains on the New York stage (not a bad idea for some of the actors we've seen). Robert Armstrong comes out and recites a synopsis of the Skull Island adventure, saying that twelve of their party met horrible deaths. Actually, the count was ten. The dinosaur overturns a raft and kills three in the water plus the man who climbs the tree. Kong kills six more when he shakes them off a long branch into a ravine. The other deaths were residents of Skull Island.

The Ocean Breeze Did Him Good

Then again, King Kong is eighteen feet tall when he's on Skull Island, built to a one-foot-to-one-inch scale. But in New York, he's twenty-four feet tall. See what an ocean cruise can do for you?

How Many Women From Where?

Then again, *Seven Women From Hell* (1961) is not the kind of horror movie that title implies. It's actually about female prisoners of war. Six of them.

I'll Bet the Guys in Precinct 13 Were Glad

Did anyone notice that the *Assault on Precinct 13* (1976) was actually an attack on Precinct 9? Yep. And was Russian director Mikhail Romm aware that his film, *The Thirteen* (1936), was supposedly about a desert patrol of thirteen soldiers—except that there were only twelve?

Maybe the Six Was Upside Down

Klaatu the alien is shot and admitted to Room 306 of Walter Reed Hospital in *The Day the Earth Stood Still* (1951). Later, when he's talking to Professor Barnhardt, he says he stayed in Room 309.

The *Godfather* Series

Here we go again, into dangerous territory. Anytime you deal with movies as popular as Francis Ford Coppola's *Godfather* series, you're flying right in the face of some fans who've watched them carefully, time and again. But the same fans have found some interesting flubbery, even in the work of a master such as Coppola. Start the theme music ...

In *The Godfather* (1972), when Michael (Al Pacino) shoots McCluskey the police chief (Sterling Hayden), and Tattaglia (Tony Giorgio), he fires at the chief's neck. McCluskey grabs his neck when the bullet hits, but in the long shot and the next close-up, the chief is bleeding from his forehead.

Also notice that at the toll booth massacre of Sonny (James Caan), the booth itself is properly aged and weathered, but a highway engineer noticed that the guard rail beside it is both new and of a modern design.

In *The Godfather Part II* (1974), as young Vito (Corleone) Andolini enters New York harbor on the ship *Moshulu*,

notice that the immigrants are standing on the side of the ship from which they would see the Statue of Liberty when they're leaving the harbor. The ship is actually going *downstream* past the Statue. That means that it's going out to sea, rather than into the harbor.

And in *The Godfather Part III* (1990), there's a problem with the papacy. The story is set in 1979, but Popes Paul VI and John Paul I figure prominently in the film; both died in 1978. In fact, a *New York Times* front page which carries an announcement of the appointment of John Paul I has a 1990 copyright date next to its March 27, 1980, publication date. Pope John Paul I was elected August 28, 1978.

MIRACULOUS HEALINGS AND WONDROUS CLEAN-UPS

Part of the natural process of making a motion picture is to film scenes out of sequence. The movie that you see on the screen is a montage of scenes that were filmed for economies of scale, scheduling, and availability of actors. Quite often much more of the story was filmed than what you see on the screen in order to fit into a specific running time. Thus all of the scenes that are planned for a specific set may well be filmed together on that set, even though they appear at different points in the film.

A car that is damaged in scene "A" might well appear on screen undamaged in scene "B." The magic of the cinematic repair job is especially evident in *Smokey and the Bandit* (1977), when the sheriff Jackie Gleason's car goes through several wrecks and mysterious restorations.

In a similar case, in *Commando* (1985), Arnold Schwarzenegger, driving Rae Dawn Chong's car, rams a yellow Porsche several times during a chase, causing it to be badly dented. Later, when he drops the bad guy

off a cliff and gets into the car and drives off, the dents have miraculously disappeared—only to reappear later. When the film ràn on
television, thousands of viewers marveled at the repair job. Earl Scheib
should do so well.

While we're at it, we should also point out that Arnold has more than
one vehicular problem in *Commando*. When he pushes a disabled pickup
truck down a hill to chase his daughter's kidnappers, white smoke emits
from its exhaust pipe. Not bad for an engine that wouldn't start. And

when he's in the mall parking garage and hits the Porsche, his wallet falls to the ground. He jumps into a red convertible and drives off without picking up the wallet. A short while later, he shows Rae Dawn Chong a picture of his daughter that is in the wallet he left on the floor of the garage.

At any rate, the nonsequential shooting schedule not only can heal dents in cars, it can clean clothes, change hairstyles, and rebuild buildings.

It's time for some testimony:

Clean Dancing

The ever-fastidious Patrick Swayze, in the final dance scene of *Dirty Dancing* (1987), jumps from the stage and makes a dramatic slide across the floor on his knees. When he stands up, the knees of his black trousers are smudged, but in the next shot, they're clean and crisply pressed.

Cleaning Up the Act of Love

Preludes to cinematic lovemaking can be a pretty messy business, yet, if properly messy, can become far more sensual than seeing the act itself. Take, for example, the famous chicken-eating scene between Joyce Redman and Albert Finney in *Tom Jones* (1963). There's never been a porn film that could convey that kind of sensuality as the pair lasciviously devour a roast chicken. You know exactly what's going to happen next, even though there's never a hint of anything vaguely pornographic. Similarly, the sequence in *Ghost* (1990) wherein Demi Moore and Patrick Swayze turn the making of a clay pot into a phallic extravaganza of love and desire. Of course, they get frightfully messy— but when they turn away from the potter's wheel to paw each other as a prelude to hopping into bed, they do so with clean hands and clothes as the clay magically disappears.

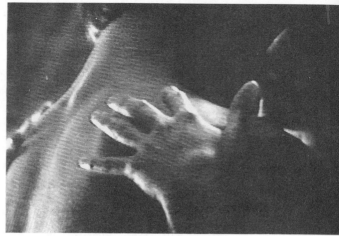

The Cleaned-Up Racer

Dave Stoller falls from his bike in the last race of *Breaking Away* (1979), and his T-shirt gets pretty dirty. But when he crosses the finish line, he has obviously stopped and changed into a fresh, clean T-shirt.

The Crane Stains

Bob Crane fights with an artist and gets paint on his suit and face in Disney's *Superdad* (1974), but the stains on both change shape and size from shot to shot.

Over the River and Through the Woods, To Grandma's Washer We Go

There must be a laundromat hidden somewhere in the woods in *Deliverance* (1972). Jon Voight decides to kill something for breakfast. While away from camp, he spots a deer, then trips and tumbles down a small hill. He's covered with leaves and dirt, but when he gets back to camp, he's clean as a whistle.

The Door to Cleanliness

Things get pretty vicious when Jim Morrison (Val Kilmer) and his girlfriend Pamela (Meg Ryan) argue at a Thanksgiving dinner in *The Doors* (1991). She throws food at him (apparently mashed yams) which splatters on his face and his clothes. As the argument continues, the mess remains on his clothes, but his face is scrubbed spotless.

A Merciful Clean-up

Kim Basinger undergoes a quick clean-up in a scene with Richard Gere in *No Mercy* (1986). In one shot she has dirt on her face, in the next she's almost clean, then dirty, then clean.

The Stainless Wife

After a battle in *Total Recall* (1990), Arnold Schwarzenegger is covered with blood. He confronts his wife (Sharon Stone), grabbing her shoulders with his bloody hands. But they leave no stains on her shoulders.

The *Rocky* Movies

Flashbacks can be a real cinematic problem, especially if they don't match the action at hand. Such was the case in *Rocky III*, wherein Rocky Balboa trains for his second bout with Clubber Lang (Mr. T) as he runs along the beach with Apollo Creed (Carl Weathers). He thinks back to their first fight, and the flashback shows Mr. T punching him in the side. Rocky is wearing the Bicentennial stars-and-stripes trunks that Apollo gave him. Wrong footage. He didn't wear them until the second fight. In the first, he was wearing yellow trunks with a black stripe.

Even though the beginning of "V" picks up where "IV" left off, in the month or so that Rocky and Adrian were in Russia, their son has aged several years and changed hair color. He also managed to change into Sly's own son, Sage Stallone.

And speaking of age, there's been much discussion over our assertion in *FILM FLUBS* that Mickey was Irish and received a Jewish funeral. We continue to contend that all indications are that the trainer (Burgess Meredith) was Irish. However, we can point out that his gravestone has him dying at the age of seventy-six, the same age as in the first movie, even though in between Rocky has aged from thirty to thirty-four and raised a small child.

And we depart the ring with word that Rocky in "V" puts an interesting spin on the wearing of his sweater. In the scene where the Balboas celebrate Christmas in the old neighborhood, Sly is wearing a white turtleneck with cable stitching down the front. When he goes down to the basement to deal with his son, the cables are gone. While he's talking to his son, the stitching's on his back. Then the cables move to the front, to the back, and to the front again.

And here's a bit of trivia for you. If you're in Los Angeles and see the Balboa Boulevard exit on the 101 Freeway, know that it's the street where Stallone lived when he was a struggling actor. Now you know where he got the family name.

NOW YOU SEE IT, NOW YOU DON'T

One of the results of stitching a film together from various non-sequential takes is that things can disappear before your eyes. Now you see it, now you don't. They're among the more amusing flubs to locate—ones that certainly make you suspend your suspension of disbelief and snap right back to reality.

More often than not, it takes a bravura flub-spotter to catch the little disappearances. They're rarely so obvious as to slap you in the face ... well, maybe they are. Let's venture into the thin air:

Somebody Licked It Off

The icing magically disappears off a cake in *Three Men and a Little Lady* (1990). Nancy Travis turns baker, tries to piece the broken cake together, and then puts chocolate icing on it. But in the next scene when she brings it to the counter all the icing is gone.

Fast Evaporation in the Summer Heat

Daryl Hannah goes up to the bar at a garden party in *Steel Magnolias* (1989), where she meets her future husband. He hands her a drink, full to the brim. When she takes it from him, however, it has lost about an inch of its contents.

He Took It Back

One of the plot points in *Gardens of Stone* (1987) is the importance to Jackie Willow (D. B. Sweeney) of the Combat Infantryman's Badge. At Willow's funeral, Hazard (James Caan) mentions this fact, then makes a great show of ripping off his own badge and placing it on the casket. But, in the next scene the badge is still pinned to Hazard's chest for the eulogy.

Lost and Found

Just before the 400-meter race in *Chariots of Fire* (1981), Jackson Schultz hands a note containing a Bible quote to Eric Liddell. He starts the race holding the note, still has it at 100 meters, but at 200 meters his spread-out fingers indicate that his hand is empty. When he goes triumphantly over the finish line, the note is again securely in his hand. Did he drop it and go back to get it? Surely not.

Ere we leave *Chariots of Fire* we should also point out that the film features one of the more persistent autograph hounds. The little girl who asks for Liddell's autograph at the meeting in East Wemyss follows him across the Firth of Forth for a gathering in Edinburgh, and is still wearing the same outfit.

And ... notice how the sweatshirts of Dennis Christopher and the American runners all bear the fifty-star flag (the one with the staggered rows of stars) back in the 1930s. A team ahead of its time.

Scared the Hat Right Off His Head

Winston (Ernie Hudson) gets his hat scared right off him in *Ghostbusters II* (1989). He, Egon (Harold Ramis) and Ray (Dan Aykroyd) are in the subway tunnel, all wearing hard hats until they are frightened by some corpseless heads and Winston's hat comes and goes as they are screaming.

Immune to the Wounds

In a dramatic scene near the end of *Lethal Weapon II* (1989), Mel Gibson shoots the bad guy five or more times in the chest as he calls out a list of names. As the man approaches him, the wounds disappear.

Losing Blood All Over the Place

John Amos gets blood all over his mouth when he and Bruce Willis fight on the wing of the airplane in *Die Hard 2* (1990). But the blood just disappears. In another fight scene, Willis gets blood on the right side of his face—but when he's on the ground laughing, the blood is, again, gone. Suddenly it reappears when he's looking for his wife.

Feats of Legerdemain

Fred Astaire was always known for his style and savoir-faire. He took it to an extreme, however, in *The Barkleys of Broadway* (1949) when, as he puts his arms around Ginger Rogers as they're riding in a cab, a lit cigarette pops into his fingers. Perhaps it's making up for the lit pipe that he put into his overcoat pocket in *Swing Time* (1936).

They Call It Vanishing Cream, Don't They?

In *Green Card* (1990), Gerard Depardieu gets a dollop of cream on his nose. (Stop me before I make a comment about that nose.) When he then comes into the room and sits down to talk to Andie MacDowell, the cream has disappeared.

Do the Right Thing, Bing

Bing Crosby lights a cigarette and starts to smoke it in *Just for You* (1952). But he must have thought better of it because the cigarette disappears in the next shot.

GoodFellas

Here we go again, catching flubs in a film that many critics—and your humble Flubmeister—consider far and above the best film of 1990. Martin Scorsese's *GoodFellas* (1990) is a lesson in all that is good in filmmaking—a strong story, fine acting, seamless directing, great cinematography. Watch it once for the story, then go back and watch it again to study how a film should be made.

But once again, we have our work to do. We have to tell you that at the beginning of the movie, it's 1963, but the boys are sitting on the back of a 1965 Chevy Impala at the airport waiting to steal a truck. At the same airport, look for a Boeing 747 taking off in the background. The airplane wasn't in use in 1963.

A tricky flub is Ray Liotta's high-speed religious conversion. Ray (as Henry Hill) is at his girlfriend's apartment when Paul Sorvino and Robert DeNiro come to talk him into going home to his wife. Notice that the cross he's wearing on his neck changes to a Star of David, then back again. We should point out that it's a plot point that he's married to a

Jewish girl and wears both the cross and Star of David on the same chain. But in this shot-to-shot sequence, there's no reason for them to change places.

While a restaurateur complains that some of the good-fellas haven't been paying their bills, wiseguy Paul Sorvino must be getting a bit flustered. As he listens, there's a huge cigar sticking out of his mouth, but in the reverse angles it isn't there.

And finally, when Lorraine Bracco drives away in the scene where she's sure that DeNiro is going to have her "whacked," the fake license plate on the car in front of her (one of the orange and blue ones formerly used in New York) falls off, revealing the current New York red, white and blue plate.

Der Flubmeister is now in serious danger of being "whacked."

A MISHMASH OF MISMATCHES

The cut from one scene to another opens a wonderful world of mismatches—scenes that simply don't connect. Something might move. Time can accelerate. Things get fixed or unfixed. Actors move from place to place. Cars get traded. Food is replenished. Welcome to the mismatch mishmash:

They Felt Bad About It, So They Fixed It

The front yard is cluttered with junk, including a white chair swing hanging from one chain, when Ron Kovic (Tom Cruise) visits the family of the man he accidentally killed in Vietnam in *Born on the Fourth of July* (1989). But while he is in the house, someone must have slipped out and fixed the swing because it's hanging from both chains when he gets back into the cab to leave.

If This Doesn't Work, Drive a Stake Through Its Heart

Near the beginning of *Casino Royale* (1967), John Huston lights his cigar as a signal for mortar fire to destroy David Niven's mansion. The place blows sky high on the first hit—then in the next it's whole again, then destroyed again.

Make Up Your Mind, Katharine!

Paul Newman takes Katharine Ross for a bicycle ride during the "Raindrops Are Falling on My Head" number in *Butch Cassidy and the Sundance Kid* (1969). She comes out of the house and sits on the handlebars of the bike; but as they ride around they're in an orchard, with Ross sitting on the crossbar in front of Newman. Then as they leave the orchard, she's back up on the handlebars again.

A Window of Opportunity

A never-say-die situation also happens in *Die Hard* (1988). Terrorists bolt a missile launcher to the ground, shatter a window as they fire it, and destroy a police car. Bad guy Alan Rickman orders them to do it again, so they fire it through the same window, shattering it once more.

Sooner or Later He'll Get It Right

Patrick Swayze can't make up his mind about his coat in *Dirty Dancing* (1987). As he and Baby (Jennifer Grey) are about to dance at the end of the movie, he first starts to take off his coat in a long shot. Then in a close-up, he once more begins removing it.

Making a Clean Breast of It

Things get pretty interesting in *Fatal Attraction* (1987) when Michael Douglas is getting dressed after making love, leaving Glenn Close still in bed. From the foot of the bed, you see Glenn's exposed breasts, then there's a cut to a side angle where the covers are up to her neck. Then it's back to the foot where she's exposed again, then to the side where she'd once more covered.

And for a bit of marathon lovemaking, notice the clock when they're at it in the kitchen. They start at 4:45, and are still at it at 6:15.

A Call to Arms

After Jamie Lee Curtis shoots the killer in the leg and he limps away in *Blue Steel* (1990), you soon see him in her bathroom pulling the bullet out bare-handed, from his arm. And notice how many shots Jamie Lee can fire from her police revolver without reloading.

Trading for the Red Wagon

When the little boy meets his foster parents for the first time in *Child's Play* 2 (1990), they're driving a gray Ford Taurus wagon. A few shots later, it's a red wagon. Did the folks trade cars?

Not-So-Close Encounters

The Richard Dreyfuss and Teri Garr encounter is not so close when they approach Devil's Tower in Steven Spielberg's *Close Encounters of the Third Kind* (1977). The two see it for the first time when they climb over an embankment, but are stopped by the military as they approach the site. The problem is that they were closer to it the first time than when they're stopped. Notice, too, how the license plate on their station wagon changes several times as they break through the roadblocks.

Spielberg is a director who loves a good inside joke—and he let the model makers build a tiny R2D2 into the Mother Ship. In *Raiders of the Lost Ark* (1981), the ubiquitous robots C3PO and R2D2 appear in the hieroglyphics on the wall when the ark is lifted up.

The Reincarnated Hamburger

We just can't leave Spielberg alone. At the beginning of *E.T.* (1982), Drew Barrymore and her mother (Dee Wallace) are eating dinner. Watch Drew's hamburger as it is restored from being half-eaten to whole, then it's gone. And when everyone's saying good-bye to E.T. at the end of the movie, in the background Mom stands up twice in less than a minute.

Green Card Greening

When Gerard Depardieu moves in with Andie McDowell in *Green Card* (1990), he removes the greens from the planter next to a bench on the balcony and substitutes vegetable seeds. Andie decides to leave the planter that way, but when she later returns from the INS interview, the greenery is back in place again.

Shifting Ships

As the liner carrying the cast passes the Statue of Liberty in *The Last of Mrs. Cheyney* (1937), the name on its bow is "Rotterdam." When Robert Montgomery talks to the purser, it becomes the "Northhampton." Later, when Joan Crawford and Frank Morgan stroll on the deck, it's the "S. S. Britain."

The Magic Pitcher

Ralph Bellamy is the catalyst for all sorts of problems with tableware. In *Pretty Woman* (1990), he's a witness to Richard Gere's disappearing sorbet dish. And in *Let's Get Married* (1937), he pours himself a glass of water by emptying a pitcher into it. Soon afterward, Reginald Denny enters the room and rouses him by dousing him from the same water pitcher. Then Ida Lupino comes into the room and pours herself a glass of water from the same pitcher.

Stock Pot-Shots

Many a moviemaker uses "stock footage"—existing film—to build a scene. Rather than go out and shoot a particular scene—especially something such as an "establishing shot" that shows a view of a city, street scenes, cloud shots, and so forth—a producer or director (or one of their flunkies) can buy the footage from a stock supplier or go back into the studio vaults. That's what special effects genius George Pal did once upon a time. However, when *War of the Worlds* (1953) and *When Worlds Collide* (1951) were shown on a double bill in the late 1950s, the audience was treated to seeing the same group of people sitting in the same store listening to the same radio telling of the approach of impending doom in both movies.

Flashback Follies

Flashbacks are a real problem when you're going back from one film to another. A director has to be on his toes to make sure that that which is recalled is that which happened in the original. If not, someone is sure to catch it (see *Rocky* flubs). In *Superman II* (1980), the flashback to Jor-El's speech about the villains General Zod, Ursa, and Non is different than it was in the original. Another flashback flub is that Superman's mother (Susannah York) places him in the earthbound capsule; his father (Marlon Brando) did it in the original.

Feats of Navigation

Lee Remick and George Segal pull off a rather amazing feat in *No Way to Treat a Lady* (1988). As they travel down the river in a police launch, they pass the Queen Mary twice, even though the launch never turns around.

Chased by the Entire Indian Nation

In *Pawnee* (1957), so much of a chase scene is made up from bits and pieces of existing footage that not only can you see color changes, but you can see different tribes of Indians doing the chasing.

To Live and Die on the Freeway

There's many a Los Angeles driver who'd like to know how the owner of a brown van pulled off an amazing feat in *To Live and Die in L.A.* (1985). In one shot, you see the van hopelessly tied up in a freeway traffic jam. But seconds later, the same van comes driving by.

Time Travel

The baby carriage scene in *The Untouchables* (1987) begins a little after 5:00, so says the clock on the wall. But it ends, three minutes later, a bit after 6:00.

Time Travel II: Slow Service at the Popcorn Stand

Mike Hammer (Ralph Meeker) goes up to a kiosk to buy popcorn in *Kiss Me Deadly* (1955). The transaction seems to take but a few seconds. However, when Mike walks up, a clock in the background shows 2:10; when he buys the popcorn it's 2:15; when he walks away, it's 2:20.

Back to the Future

Granted, when you're dealing with a trilogy such as the *Back to the Future* movies (two of which were made back-to-back), there are more than enough possibilities for error. In the first place, there are time shifts within each movie, then there are time shifts back and forward to previous and future films. Add flashbacks and flash forwards to the mix—and the shooting of "II" and "III" at the same time, and you have the recipe for disaster. It's a tribute to director Robert Zemeckis, writer Bob Gale, and everyone else involved that they were able to keep their wits about them. But…there were a few slips, and flub-spotters caught them.

Let's see. In the original, Marty McFly (Michael J. Fox) goes into a diner in 1965, and pays for his coffee with change from his pocket. He should be glad that the cashier didn't look too closely at it, since it would be 1985 money.

There's a real time shift when Marty jumps into the DeLorean to escape the Libyan terrorists. The odometer

mileage is at first 33061 then it zaps back to 32904 a few seconds later. Sounds like what happened in *Smokey and the Bandit* (1977) where the mileage on Burt Reynolds Trans-Am never changes. Never buy a used car from a movie studio.

Fans of TV's *The Honeymooners* know their show so well that several caught a flub when Marty visits his *Back to the Future* mother-yet-to-be. It's November 5, 1955, yet they're watching an episode with Jackie Gleason and Art Carney entitled "The Man From Space." That episode first aired on December 31, 1955.

When Doc (Christopher Lloyd) is hanging from the clock near the end of the film, he's wearing sneakers with Velcro straps. Velcro wasn't invented until 1967, and didn't appear on shoes until a few years later.

Marty McFly writes a note to Doc about his future demise on dinner stationery. Doc tears up the note, but in the last scene, after he's been saved from a hail of gunfire by his bulletproof vest, he hands the taped-up note back to Marty. But the restored note is on different stationery.

When Marty does his guitar riff on the high school stage, the giant amplifier blows him into a bookshelf filled with paper, all of which falls on him. In the long shots, it's all on Marty. In the subsequent close-ups, more paper is seen falling.

And finally, we have to wonder if Texaco paid some bucks to join the mass of advertisers who bought on-screen "product placement" time in "II." Doc stuffs garbage into the DeLorean, signifying that in the future there's no need for gasoline. Yet later, in the future, we see a modern-looking Texaco station. Do they pump gas or garbage?

FOLEY FOOLISHNESS

When he decided to go into the sound effects branch of the movie business, Universal's Ed Foley turned out to be such a pioneer that he joined the ranks of Kilroy, Murphy, Sandwich, Volt, Ampere, Boycott, Diesel, Bloomer, Crapper, and all the other worthies whose family name has gone into the language—on one hand immortalizing them, on the other stripping them of their status as real life human beings.

Foley gave his name to sound effects recording, and these days you see Foley editor, Foley artist, and Foley stages listed the in the credits of most films.

Foley work is part of the "sweetening" process. Often, the actual sound that's recorded isn't the one our ears are trained to hear, or isn't sufficient to carry the moment in the film. We're so ear-trained by the movies that the "real" sound of a thunderstorm doesn't register as well as a soundman's artificial thunder sheet. Likewise with a fight—the real-life sound of punching and smacking differs from what we hear on screen, whereas the onscreen sound seems like reality.

I recall reading that in *Apocalypse Now* (1979) the actual noise of the helicopters didn't sound right on the track, so it was replaced with an effect created by some chains in a paper bag. Of course, the most frightening sound in that movie, Wagner's *Ride of the Valkyries*, which heralded the silent approach of the helicopters, was produced without Foley devices.

The Foley artist reaches into his bag of cinematic tricks to create all kinds of noises—airplane engines, horse hoofbeats, footsteps, windstorms, car crashes, etc.

For example: take breaking glass. On the set, any glass that breaks is probably going to be what the special effects artists call "candy glass," once made from melted sugar. When an actor goes through a prop window, it will not make too much noise—until the Foley editor puts it onto the sound track.

Similarly, in a fight scene, it's a rare actor who wants to take an actual punch (and a rarer insurance company that will allow it). As a result, the camera is set up so that the actors can aim a punch and score a near miss, with the air space eliminated by the camera's depth of field. The corresponding "thud" probably comes from a Foley artist slugging a rump roast or some similar material for the soundtrack. Most of the time you don't know the difference. But, if you're one of the flub spotters who noticed, in *The Godfather* (1972), that even though one punch misses its intended recipient by a country mile, the thud is there anyway.

As much as they enhance the workings of a film, there are times when the Foley work goes awry. For example: When a car roars off and/or spins out on a dirt road, we hear the tires screeching. On a dirt road? Come on! More cases:

Foley to the Second Power

What we have here is a Foley/Foley situation. When Eddie Murphy, as Axel Foley, goes to the gun club in *Beverly Hills Cop II* (1987), he watches the "six-foot blond" (Brigitte Nielsen) using the firing range for target

shooting with a pistol. However, each time the gun fires, you hear a "blam, tinkle, tinkle," indicating that her spent cartridges are falling to the floor. From a pistol?

It's Not Jake With Us

Big Jake's (John Wayne) son Michael (Chris Mitchum) rides a very old motorcycle in the Western, *Big Jake* (1971). In fact, a biking enthusiast pointed out that this motorcycle is one of the first ever produced, perhaps a very old Harley Davidson. But the sound is that of a modern Japanese bike. And in a close-up, you can see that the old American bike is powered by a very modern Japanese engine.

It's Not Jake II (The Two Jakes)

Likewise, near the end of *Black Rain* (1989), another motorcycle enthusiast, with an ear for that sort of thing, reported that Michael Douglas and a bad guy are chasing through a field on two-stroke, one-cylinder dirt bikes. But the sound is that of a four-stroke motor.

One Hell of an Echo

Nick and Nora Charles are at a nightclub celebrating New Year's Eve in *After the Thin Man* (1936), where a chanteuse is singing "Smoke Dreams." After finishing, she is seen leaving the club with a man. A few scenes later, Nick and Nora are in the owner's office using the telephone, and just as the sequence ends, you can hear the chanteuse still singing "Smoke Dreams," even though she previously had left the club.

Oklahoma Crude...Really Crude

Excuse us for a moment of crudity. In *Oklahoma Crude* (1973), director Stanley Kramer must have opted to yield to the MPAA ratings mavens rather than stick to the script as recorded. Faye Dunaway is talking to George C. Scott over a meal. Scott taunts her for being tough and masculine. He asks her if she'd prefer having a man's genitals or a woman's. She replies, "Both." Then he sets himself up by asking "Why?" Now watch her lips as she says, "Because if I had both, I could fuck myself." But that's not what you'll hear. To appease the MPAA, Kramer had Dunaway loop the line to say "screw myself." But the lips don't lie.

Yo, Olivia! We Can't Hear You!

When Michael Beck and Gene Kelly are conversing up close during the reconstruction of the auditorium in *Xanadu* (1980), the camera shows Olivia Newton-John talking to them off in the distance, but you don't hear a word. The two turn and say something to her. Did someone on the crew forget to turn on her mike?

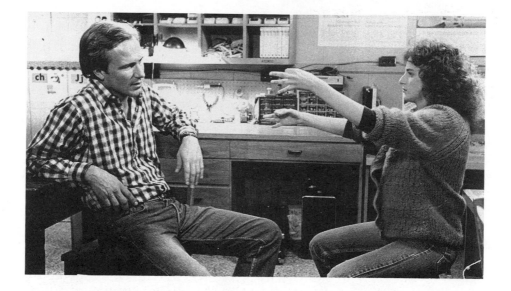

Dirty Hands

And while we're at it, what was going on in *Walker* (1988) to cause Marlee Matlin to sign "Fuck off"? We didn't catch it, but an alert gaffe spotter who could read sign language did. And another reports that in *Children of a Lesser God* (1986), filmed while Matlin and William Hurt were real-life lovers, there are times that the sign language conversation is not about the plot of the film, but idle chatter between the two about things going on in their offscreen life.

The Not-So-Silent Scream

Christopher Reeve bursts in on Michael Caine and Dyan Cannon in their bedroom in *Deathtrap* (1982) and Cannon screams. She screams so long, in fact, that when they go to a three-shot, she's still screaming even though her mouth is closed.

An Attack of English Amidst the Din

In the 1939 classic *Gunga Din*, the natives, none of whom speak English, are fighting. Yet within all the noise of battle, you can hear one of them yell "watch out" in perfect English.

IN THE TIME TUNNEL

For some of us, anachronisms are the most difficult thing to spot in a film; for others, the easiest. When something's out of its proper time frame, unless we have an expertise, the boo-boo passes on by, sans notice. But there's one thing you have to think of when you're making a film. Out there in the vast audience, there are always people who know their fields, whether it's music, art, automobiles, philately, whatever.

There are times when it's downright amazing. A philatelist noticed that in *The Two Jakes* (1990), a stamp on a letter that Jack Nicholson picks up came along about a year after the time of the movie. He could tell by the color of the stamp. Another noticed that one of the letters that Indy picks up in his father's study has a stamp on it that commemorates a hundred years of Texas statehood, one that was issued seven years *after* the time of the film.

A collector of Coca-Cola memorabilia pointed out that young George Bailey (later played by Jimmy Stewart) in *It's a Wonderful Life* (1946) works in a drugstore, and the narration indicates that he's "twelve years old in 1919." But he's standing next to a Coca-Cola thermometer—"the Silhouette Girl"—which wasn't produced until 1938.

Music is a real bugaboo. Those keen of ear and sharp of eye can always spot a song out of its time—whether (as pointed out in *FILM FLUBS*) it's "The Man That Got Away," crooned a mere twenty years before it was written by a saloon chanteuse to a young Lee in the 1988 *Liberace* TV mess of a movie, or other songs that were released not all that long after the movie's time frame—e.g., "Stop in the Name of Love," released in 1965 and "Reach Out (in the Name of Love)," released in 1966, in *Cooley High* (1975), which takes place in 1964.

Into the time tunnel:

Not So Cool

In *Air America* (1990), set in the late 1960s, you can hear "Long Cool Woman," released in 1973.

Altered Time

Ken Russell's *Altered States* (1980) is set in 1967, but in the exterior shots you can see VW Rabbits, Plymouth Volares, and other 1970s cars.

Trading Cars in Beverly Hills

Eddie Murphy's Ferrari changes from an early eighties model to a late eighties model (different wheels and front bumper) in *Beverly Hills Cop II* (1987). Later, two men in a mid-eighties Camero are ordered to kill Murphy, but when they go to carry out the deed, they're in a 1978 or 1979 Camero. A car aficionado noticed.

Dances With History

Kevin Costner's *Robin Hood: Prince of Thieves* (1991)—a.k.a. "Dances With Peasants"—dances around historical accuracy in several instances. Most notable is the use of gunpowder by Azeem (Morgan Freeman). Given that the film is set in the late 1100s, we have to remember that Marco Polo, who found gunpowder in China and brought it to the West, wasn't born until 1254 and didn't even begin his trek eastward until around 1271. The Amazing Azeem sinned again with his use of a crude telescope. Its inventor, Galileo, didn't come along until 1564. And as for the use of the word "twit," we don't think it was a word common to the era of Robin and his merry band, since it came into the language in the 1920s. And about those "wanted" posters—How were they printed, given that Gutenberg wouldn't get around to inventing the printing press for another 200 years?

Sneaking Into the Future

In Oliver Stone's *Born on the Fourth of July* (1989), one of the Vietnam-era vets is wearing Reebok sneakers in a scene set in 1972 at the Chicago Democratic Convention. Reeboks didn't come around until 1978.

Future Farmers

The Color Purple (1985) is set in 1938–39. One of the tractors on the farm has rubber tires, which weren't introduced to farming until 1945.

The Future Is in the Background

In the 1983 Spanish production of *Carmen*, the time frame of course, is the 1800s. As the gypsies dance around the campfire, the lights of Seville brighten in the background as a helicopter arrives with its landing lights blazing.

Flying Through a Time Warp

In filming the Japanese-American war epic, *Tora! Tora! Tora!* on Oahu in 1970, Japanese planes fly over KoleKole Pass, west of the Schofield Barracks en route to Pearl Harbor. In a rare irony, they fly right over a white cross memorializing the soldiers who were strafed by the Zeroes as they approached Pearl Harbor, the first casualties of the war. In the background you can see Tripler Army Hospital, built after the war in 1945.

Power Failure

In 1935's *Great Impersonation*, Edmund Lowe is seen going to bed by candlelight in an old English country house. But when he is awakened during the night, there's an electric light switch nearby.

Not So Young and Gay

The word "gay" is heard all through *Victor/Victoria* (1982). The film takes place in the 1930s and "gay," as a pseudonym for homosexual, hadn't yet come into common use.

Nuclear Accidents

Those Magnificent Men in Their Flying Machines (1965) takes place in 1910, but in the scene where Terry-Thomas has his airplane stuck between two cars of a moving freight train, you can see a nuclear power plant in the background. And in *Yanks* (1979), Richard Gere plays a World War II G.I. in love with Britisher Lisa Eichhorn. As they take a stroll through the English countryside there, in the background, is yet another nuclear power station.

Modern Medicine in Ancient Rome

The newly re-released *Spartacus* (1960) is a marvel of film restoration and a lesson in epic filmmaking. Having seen it perfectly projected on a massive screen, we aren't too sure about what we thought were tennis shoes and wristwatches on some Roman soldiers in the battle scenes, as reported in *FILM FLUBS* They certainly looked like it on video, but blown up it appears that things are kosher. We await refutation. However, we did get a couple of giggles—one being evidence of modern medicine in ancient Italy. When Kirk Douglas is first brought into Peter Ustinov's gladiator school, notice the very prominent vaccination mark on his arm. Shortly before that, when Ustinov is out scouting for gladiator stock, you get a quick flash of his Jockey shorts as he dismounts from his steed.

126

Precursor to a Disaster

At the beginning of *Wall Street* (1987), we're told that it begins in the winter of 1985. However, in an opening scene one stockbroker tells another that Gordon Gekko (Michael Douglas) was selling NASA shares ten minutes after the Challenger disaster—which took place in January 1986.

Talk About a Sneak Preview!

This hurts. This really hurts. Your humble scribe's favorite movie of the last however many years—perhaps favorite movie of a lifetime of filmgoing—is flawed. In a scene set in postwar Sicily in *Cinema Paradiso* (1989), the young projectionist watches a scene from *And God Created Woman*. A calendar shows you that it's 1954. That Bardot classic was released in 1957.

But we don't care. *Cinema Paradiso* is still one of the loveliest movies ever made about he movies—a real valentine to the world of cinema.

Who's Watching the Store?

In the movie *Three Little Words* (1950), a poster for the Marx Brothers' 1928 Broadway show *Animal Crackers* uses a publicity still from MGM's *The Big Store* (1941).

Another Shorts Story

The prehistoric man that is thawed back to life in *Return of the Ape Man* (1944) is wearing cotton underwear beneath his animal skin loincloth.

Star Trek

Perhaps we should don a suit of armor. We're going to talk about a series of films with devotees who know them frame by frame. Stand back—we're going to talk about the *Star Trek* movies.

Elsewhere in *SON OF FILM FLUBS*, you'll find some notation of flubs in the *Star Trek* TV series. There is, of course, a bit of crossover between the two, one instance of which produced a TV-to-film flub (see page 139). However, since we're dealing with film here, we'll keep them separate.

We have quite a few Trekkies (or is it Trekkers? We've heard that one term is acceptable, one isn't, so forgive us if we err) who were more than happy to share their favorites. Beam us up, Scotty.

In *Star Trek—The Motion Picture* (1979), there's a scene where Spock is floating around outside the Enterprise. Kirk has discovered that Spock is gone, and leaves the ship through an airlock. The close-ups show Kirk floating away from the ship, then in the next shot, if you look carefully you

129

can see the ceiling of the soundstage, with interior stage walls to the right and left. The camera has pulled back too far. (See notes on framing, pages 20-23).

In *Star Trek II: The Wrath of Khan* (1982), when told that Spock is dying, Kirk runs to the engine room with his jacket buttoned all the way up. But when he reaches the engine room, it's opened all the way back with the white flaps showing. Then when he gets to the glass, one lapel shows with the red side of the other jacket buttoned across it. When he slides to the floor, both white jacket flaps show again.

Also notice that Kirk is given a pair of antique glasses, later dated in *Star Trek IV* to be from the eighteenth century. But the ear pieces are modern clear plastic.

In *Star Trek IV: The Voyage Home* (1986), watch a young nun standing by the aquarium as she inexplicably changes into an older nun. Also, in the scene were Sulu pilots a helicopter carrying a large crate, watch the changing position of the plastic between the time he flies toward San Francisco and lowers it onto the Klingon ship.

And finally, in *Star Trek V: The Final Frontier* (1989), watch the changing colors of Shatner's tunic when he falls from El Capitan Mountain. It's blue when he falls and black in the close-ups. Was there a mismatch in the blue screen effect?

But the flub most noticed in all the *Star Trek* movies was a problem with the elevator shaft in "V." Watch as they pass the same floor several times on their way up. It's 35, 52, 64, 52, 77, 78, and 78 again.

TV TROUBLES

The flub-finding challenge is magnified when a dedicated spotter catches something in a television program. Most television shows are with us for a fleeting moment, then vanish into the ether until years later when they come back time and again and again in syndication. Occasionally, a flubbed TV movie will emerge on home video, but most either go back into the vaults or head for foreign shores as theatrical features.

However, we do get the chance to look for the flubs that we think we saw when a program re-emerges in syndication or when, as in the case of the *I Love Lucy, Star Trek, The Fugitive,* and *The Twilight Zone*, it becomes a cult favorite and appears not only day after day on your home screen, but also in videocassettes and laserdisc versions.

Devotees of these shows, having seen them time and again, find their little flaws and love to share them among themselves. Several have generously supplied their favorite gaffes to *SON OF FILM FLUBS*, giving us the rare opportunity to delve into television flubdom.

The Wet Address—and Other "Lucy" Flubs

At the risk of besmirching an icon, our first look is at the wonderful *I Love Lucy* series. We're on fairly solid ground here, since the *Lucy* flubs were supplied by Bart Andrews, perhaps the world's leading authority on

the work of Lucille Ball, author of three books on her, and consultant to Universal Studios on their *I Love Lucy* tribute attraction.

"There's a blooper or two in just about every one of the 179 episodes," Andrews says, and he shares his favorites.

He reports that if you go to New York to look for the Ricardo's home, you might need scuba gear. In the series, Lucy and Desi lived at 623 East 68th Street. That particular location happens to be in the middle of the East River.

Even more fun is finding all of Ethel's middle names. "Ethel Mertz had three different middle names," Bart reports, "the result of overworked scriptwriters who didn't have time to go back and check previous scripts. For trivia buffs, the middle monikers were Louise, Mae, and Vivian Vance's real middle name, Roberta."

How about the time that the Ricardos moved a few doors down the hall without really changing apartments? The writers surreptitiously changed Lucy and Ricky's apartment number from 3-B to 3-D so they could make a joke about three-dimensional movies. But when the episode was over, the new number remained on the apartment door.

Lucy teaches Ethel to drive in an episode which comes a couple of years *after* one in which Ethel talks about following Lucy in a station wagon.

"More than once," Bart adds, "a musician in Desi Arnaz's orchestra would refer to the leader as 'Desi,' not 'Ricky.' Rather than do expensive retakes, they'd decided to just let it slide, justifying their decision by probably reasoning that TV would probably be a fleeting fad."

The Set Designer Was No Hero

It's set in World War II, of course, and in an episode of *Hogan's Heroes*, Colonel Hogan (Bob Crane) is secretly flown to England during the night, just before D-Day. In the background, there's map showing both East and West Germany— a split that didn't happen until after the war.

The Fugitive—Running Away From His Flubs

Finally, we dissect *The Fugitive* TV series—one which has also taken on cult status. We have fan Linda Rogers to thank for a list of things that bothered her in the series:

The numerous writers couldn't agree on whether fugitive Richard Kimble's wife (whom he had been convicted of killing) had been strangled or bludgeoned, even though the flashbacks at the beginning of each program show that she was hit with a lamp. In the final episode the one-armed man confirms that he hit her.

The time frame seems to indicate that Kimble was indeed an over-achiever. Let's see if we can add it up: When his wife is killed, he is thirty-three. By that time, according to various episodes, he has completed college, medical school, an internship, two residencies, and two years in Korea as a medic, and built up a successful practice. Let's see—if he got out of college at twenty-two (assuming he started at eighteen), then had four years of medical school, that's twenty-six. Then a year of internship—twenty-seven; two residencies at two years each (guess)—thirty-one; two years in Korea—thirty-three. So when did he get around to starting the practice?

The Fugitive stops at the Edmund Hotel in Kansas City, Sioux Falls, and various other cities. Was it a national chain, or an inside joke?

In a first-season two-parter, the title word twice is misspelled "Lonley."

In the final episode, Kimble and the one-armed man duke it out atop a ride in an abandoned amusement park—beside which is a healthy palm tree. Even though the ride is called "Mahi Mahi," can a palm tree survive in Indiana?

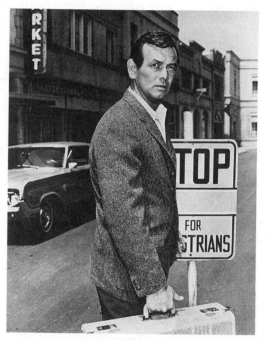

The Fugitive, with a wounded Norma Crane in tow, runs all over the place to escape the police in episode 56, finally ending up in a construction hut. Along the way he changes socks several times, from light to dark. Now, that's being fastidious. But after all, he's a doctor trained in hygiene. Of course, he doesn't wash his hands until *after* he performs kitchen surgery in episode 103.

In episode 106 there's a tense moment when guest star John Larch calls his son (Beau Bridges) by the name that the Fugitive is using.

And we conclude on a more intimate note: In the first place, throughout the series, David Janssen is forever tripping on things, stumbling, backing into things, and having near-misses which, perhaps, can be attributed to his oft-reported heavy drinking and his bum leg. Of course, most of the dangerous work was done by a stunt man who bore very little resemblance to Janssen other than being male.

Our faithful correspondent also noticed that in episode 93, something might well have been going on in the dressing room trailer between takes. She thought that he was walking down the street with a golf ball in the left front pocket of his polyester pants. But she called in her husband, himself a golfer of the polyester pants generation, who took a look at the tape and pointed out that it was no golf ball—it was certainly an aroused actor. Sorta recalls the old Mae West line from *She Done Him Wrong* (1933)—"Is that a gun in your pocket, or are you just glad to see me?"

Were They Having a Shaving Cream Fight?

In an episode of *Moonlighting*—one which, oddly enough, won the Emmy for editing—Davis Addison (Bruce Willis) runs into Maddie's (Cybill Shepherd) office in an undershirt and red and white boxers with shaving cream on his face. In the subsequent banter the shaving cream is alternately spread over his face or mostly wiped off.

137

Miss-M*A*S*H'es

In one episode of the popular TV series, *M*A*S*H*, a wounded G.I. shoots a Chinese soldier who is trying to steal boots. Later they become friends at the 4077th, where the American gives the enemy soldier a Hershey Bar as a gesture of friendship. The candy bar has a bar code on the wrapper—a computerization phenomenon that wasn't around until decades after the Korean War.

And in another episode, Colonel Blake is on the phone talking about the movies that they are showing. He says, "We only got *The Thing* and *The Blob*." The Korean War lasted from 1950 to 1953; they may well have had *The Thing*, since it was released in 1951. But *The Blob* didn't ooze out until 1958.

The Search for the Right Skyline

Manhunt: The Search for the Night Stalker (1989) is a made-for-TV movie which takes place in Los Angeles during a 1985 serial murder case. In the background, you can see the newly built Library Tower (okay, it's really the First Interstate World Center, but no red-blooded Angeleno calls it by that corporate gobbledygook). It's the tallest building in the West, but was nowhere near completion in 1985.

Where Wise Men Fear to Trek

Deal with a series as popular as both the TV and film emanations of *Star Trek* , with its legions of fans who know each episode frame by frame, and you're sure to do some Trekkie toe treading. Actually, many of the devotees of the series came forward to share their favorite *Star Trek* flubs. Glitches and goof-ups from the *Trek* films are dealt with elsewhere in this book. But now it's time to take a look at the TV series. Fools rush in...

In an episode entitled "The Alternative Factor," notice how actor Robert Brown's goatee ranges from grown to partially grown to sparse with just a few strands of hair.

Leonard Nimoy is seen meditating in a close-up in the "Amok Time" episode. A cut to a wide shot shows him casually leaning against the wall in the background, then the next cut shows him meditating again.

The crew is attacked by a World War II fighter in "Shoreleave." When the plane is first seen, it's a U. S. Navy Corsair (recognizable by its gull-wing configuration and U. S. military markings). In the close-ups, the plane is a Japanese Zero.

As Guinan (Whoopi Goldberg) and Geordie (LeVar Burton) play chess in the *Star Trek: The Next Generation* episode "Galaxy's Child," the camera angles change, and so do the numbers and positions of the pieces on the 3-D chess board.

The *Indiana Jones* Movies

The Indiana Jones movies—*Raiders of the Lost Ark* (1981), *Indiana Jones and the Temple of Doom* (1984), and *Indiana Jones and the Last Crusade* (1989)—offer many opportunities for flub-finding fun. Their being action-adventure films means that there's much going on and many opportunities to slip up. Into the fray:

In the beginning, Indy and a Mexican man are in a cave. Indy says, "Adios, Sapito." The character is "Saripo" in the credits and "Satipo" in the novel.

When Indy's enemy Beloq and a group of German soldiers escort the Ark to a place on the island to open it, Indy shows up with a missile launcher. Beloq says, "You give mercenaries a bad name." Then a fly gives Beloq a bad taste as it lands on his face, and appears to crawl into his mouth. Did he eat it? Wonder if it's the same live-action fly which appears in the "Dance of the Hours" scene in Disney's animated *Fantasia* (1940). Does it have a SAG card?

140

A special effect goes awry when Indy faces the hooded cobra. There's a brief flash of light which reflects on the glass partition that separates our hero from the deadly snake. Really. Just like the one that comes between Cary Grant and the leopard which he finds in the bathroom in *Bringing Up Baby* (1938).

The Temple of Doom is safe from our examination for now. We'll move on the *The Last Crusade* where, early on, young Indy (River Phoenix) is in a rail car and grabs the whip—

soon to be his trademark—to fend off a lion. He cuts himself with the whip, which explains the origin of the scar that he carries on his chin for the rest of his life. But the cut on his chin runs from right to left, and on Harrison Ford it slants left to right. (Ford got the real scar in an auto accident while trying to fasten his seat belt.)

Indy arrives at his father's (Sean Connery) ransacked house and finds that Dad is missing. He picks up his father's mail, then puts it down. But when he opens Dad's diary, he's still holding the mail.

We talked about he "blood switch" on young Indy's chin in *FILM FLUBS*, so we find that it's incumbent to report that it happens again on the ship when Indy is beaten up in the rainstorm. Blood is on one side of his mouth, he hangs his head, and when he looks up, the blood has moved to the other side. During the truck chase, scaffolding and boulders fall on its roof mangling the roof rack—but the rack's back again, miraculously repaired, when the Nazi crawls over the roof.

When Indy's in the library talking to the wealthy backer, watch as both the amount of champagne in the glass and the position of his arm jump around as the film editor cut from shot to shot.

Indy and his father ride in the German zeppelin *Hindenberg*. The scene takes place in 1938. The *Hindenberg* disaster was in 1937.

A bit of model-maker inaccuracy: Inside the tank, there's plenty of passage between the body and the turret. But when it goes over a cliff and is destroyed, the turret comes off, revealing a solid top and the peg which holds it on.

When Indy's in the library and sees the giant "X" on the floor, marking the burial site of the Knight of the Grail, notice how when he sees the "X" from the balcony, the floor changes color as he gets down; but, more importantly, the "X" fades and disappears as he begins breaking through the floor.

Finally, the powers of the "Cup of Christ" are revealed when Indy uses it to heal his father's wound. He empties the cup onto the wound, turning it upside down, but when his father looks into it, there's about an inch of water therein.

BACKGROUND BRIEFING

It's the things which go on in the foreground that moviemakers want you to see, with the background merely providing the frame for same. But should your eye wander from that which is supposed to be the center of your attention, you just might find film flubs creeping in off in yon distance. Take a look at some of the things you can see, when you watch the big picture:

She's Ba-a-ack!

They just can't get rid of Cher in one scene of *Silkwood* (1983). In the latter part of the film, when the house is plundered by the men searching for radiation, Karen (Meryl Streep) and Dolly (Cher) are questioned, then Dolly is escorted into a waiting car an taken away. But not long afterward, in a close shot of Karen, you can see Dolly slightly out of focus, still in the background.

Glasnost Take the Hind Most

In *Rambo III* (1988), Sly Stallone steals a Russian "Hind" helicopter just after he releases his Green Beret commander (Richard Crenna) and some Afghan rebels from their cells. Watch as the "Russian" helicopter revs up and you'll see a small American flag on its rotor housing.

145

A Dangerous Business

Show business is a painful business for one of the dancers in *There's No Business Like Show Business* (1954). During the "Heat Wave" number, Marilyn Monroe accidentally hits one of the male dancers across the face with her hand.

Getting Glare in Your Eyes

Early in the classic Western *Shane* (1953), Alan Ladd is riding across a field. In the distance is a fast-moving glare, obviously the sun reflecting from the windshield of a speeding car. In the same film, look for Elisha Cook, Jr.'s body to move around from shot to shot as he lies dead in the mud.

High Noon in Hollywood

There's a crane shot in *High Noon* (1952) that starts with Gary Cooper and pans up to show the empty streets. But the camera pulls back a bit too far, and you see beyond that set to telephone poles in the background. And, by the way, did anyone notice the changing of the town newspaper? Sometimes it's the *Chronicle*, at others it's the *Clarion*.

Perhaps He Should Stick Out His Thumb

While a pursued Cornel Wilde searches for food in darkest Africa in *The Naked Prey* (1966), a car drives by in the background. (Just a thought: With the change of just one letter, this title could become a movie about Sunday morning in a nudist colony.)

Sneak Preview

"Product Placement" has become a near and dear technique in modern moviemaking. This is the prominent display of products in a film, providing the manufacturer has ponied up a hunk of change for the privilege. Nowhere is it more prominent than in Universal's *Back to the Future* trilogy, films which are at times one long commercial. But Warner Bros. is not without the stain of sin. In the 1990 *My Blue Heaven*, a theater marquee in the background advertises Warner's *White Hunter, Black Heart*, the Clint Eastwood film to be released later in the year.

Not as Deserted as You Think

A long shot in *Mysterious Island* (1961) establishes that when a hot-air balloon is downed, the cast is on a deserted island—deserted except for a crewman who darts behind a rock in the background.

A Shot in the Dark

When the punks drive up to a house enroute to terrorize the occupants early in Stanley Kubrick's chilling *A Clockwork Orange* (1971), watch as a crew person darts out of the shot in the dark background.

Home Alone

We are troubled. We are greatly troubled. We are bothered that a simple little movie called *Home Alone* (1990) has become, as of this writing, the fourth largest-grossing movie in cinematic history. It's a pleasant time-passer with a cute kid and some funny bad guys—essentially a live-action version of a Road Runner/Wile E. Coyote cartoon. But up there in the stratosphere with *E.T.*, *Gone With the Wind*, and the others? Wow. We despair as to what it says about today's audiences.

That being said, you can understand that we take particular delight in issuing a few jabs:

When pint-sized Macauley Culkin's mom (Catherine O'Hara) is frantically trying to get back from Orly Airport in Paris, it's obvious that the scene was filmed in another airport (apparently O'Hare in Chicago). You can see the tail of an Eastern Airlines DC-9 is in the background. Eastern doesn't fly to Paris (in fact, it doesn't fly at all anymore), but if it did, it wouldn't be in a DC-9, a short-range aircraft designed for domestic use.

149

Also when Mom leaves Paris, she departs on a American Airlines 767, and arrives on an American 757. Did she change planes along the way?

When the kid goes to the grocery, he buys Tide detergent among his other provisions. But at the end of the film, when he tells his mom exactly what he bought, he says that he bought fabric softener. He didn't.

And the wonderful Joe Pesci has a real problem with the hot doorknob. He grabs it with his right hand, then clutches his left hand with his right in pain, then he plunges the right hand into the snow. When he looks at the burned hand, the initial burned into it is upside down in relation to the way he grabbed the knob.

ENDNOTE

The response from readers of *FILM FLUBS* was both awesome and gratifying. Literally hundred of letters poured in, amazing us with the time and trouble that was taken to list favorite flubs, and delighting us with flub-spotting discoveries. The volume of mail has truly been overwhelming.

We've tried to keep up with all of the wonderful people who contributed to this effort, and names are listed with grateful thanks, in our "Sharp-Eyed, Quick-Witted Flubs Spotter" list. Quite often, we received multiple letters about a particular flub, and, while we try to list all who wrote us, there may be some omissions. Also we'd like to acknowledge all of the people we know by first name only who called in to share their favorites with Der Flubmeister on radio and TV talk shows from coast to coast. If we missed your name, please let us know, and it will be acknowledged in future editions. In addition, there were so many people who stopped us on the street to relay a favorite, or friends who told us of flubs over the telephone. Hopefully, they're listed here. If not, *mea maxima culpa*. Forgive me. The situation will be rectified.

The majority of letters and radio call-in questions which came after the publication of *FILM FLUBS* asked, "When can we expect a sequel?" Well, here it is. The fantastic reception to the book has certainly encouraged us to keep this series going—and we'd love for you to be a part of it. Tell us about your favorite film fumbles. Write:

FILM FLUBS
7510 Sunset Boulevard, #551
Hollywood, CA 90046

Your contribution may well become a part of *FILM FLUBS III: THE ADVENTURE CONTINUES!*

Bill Givens
Hollywood, California
June 1991

A BRIEF GLOSSARY OF TERMS USED IN "SON OF FILM FLUBS"

[A]TION: The events that happen in front of the camera; third in [the] classic sequence of "Lights…camera…action!" Also the direc[tor's] call to start the scene moving.

[AN]AMORPHIC: A lens that compresses a wide-angle picture onto [stan]dard film stock. When projected through another anamorphic [lens], the picture is "unsqueezed" back to normal proportions. You often see this effect when a film shot anamorphic is shown on [tele]vision. The title sequences are often left "squeezed," since they [wou]ld have to be completely redone for the television format. So [you] get tall, stretched people in the shot.

[ASP]ECT RATIO: The width-to-height ratio of the projected [mo]tion picture frame. For example, the "Academy" ratio is 1.33 to [1, "]Standard" ratio is 1.85:1, and "Wide-Screen" is 2.35:1. The [asp]ect ratio of the human eye is roughly 1.85:1.

[BE]ST BOY: The assistant chief electrician (Best Boy/Electric) or [the] assistant chief grip (Best Boy/Grip). You wondered, now you [kno]w.

[CA]N: Storage for the completed footage; "in the can" means that a [scen]e or entire film has been completed.

[CO]NTINUITY: Progression of the film's action from shot to shot. [Th]e continuity director or script supervisor keeps track of the [film]'s continuity.

[CR]EDITS: The list of people who worked on the film and their [job]s. Credits are split into "front credits," which list key players, [dir]ectors and executives at the beginning of the film, and "end [cre]dits," which normally cover everyone from the stars and the [tech]nicians to the person who brings the doughnuts and coffee to [the] set (Craft Services, if you didn't already know). The end credits [run] across the screen in a credit crawl; the front credits rarely [cra]wl. In the good old movie days, all the credits were right up [fron]t on eight or nine cards. This all changed with *Superman* and [its] twelve-minute end credit crawl of literally hundreds of names.

DAILIES (also called RUSHES): The film footage shot during one day is usually processed and viewed on the next by the key people involved with the production—usually the producer, director, cinematographer, script supervisor and film editor. This gives them the opportunity to look for technical problems, as well as to check performances and line readings by the actors.

DEPTH OF FIELD: The depth of focus in a film. If the foreground is in focus and the background blurry, the film as a "short depth of field." If the entire picture, foreground and background, is in sharp focus, the shot has a "long depth of field."

DOLLY: The wheeled platform that holds the camera and the camera operator. Due to the way it can move either forward or side-to-side, the dolly is usually called a "crab dolly." The worker who physically moves it around is called the "dolly grip."

ESTABLISHING SHOT: Normally, a wide-angle shot of a room or outdoor setting to orient the viewer to the location where the action is taking place, and often to establish a mood. Frequently called a "long shot."

FLASHBACK: A backwards jump in the time of the action, usually used to clarify a plot point or explain a situation—or, in some cases, to pad the film and drag out the action.

FOLEY: Named for Universal Studios sound effects master, "Foley" is the addition of sound effects (horses' hooves, automobile engine sounds, etc.) to the sound track. A "Foley Stage" is the sound effects studio; a "Foley Artist" creates the sound effects.

FRAME: An individual picture that, when projected at the usual twenty-four frames per second, creates—due to "persistence of vision"—the illusion of movement on the screen. As a verb, "frame" means to compose the image in the camera's viewfinder. In other words, the director or cinematographer "frames" what you will see on the screen.

FRAMING: the centering of the picture on the screen.

GAFFER: The chief electrician on a film set (bet you always wondered who that was, didn't you!).

GRIP: A physical laborer on a movie set; similar to a stagehand, but don't tell that to his or her union.

HOT SET: A set that is actively being used for filming, or is ready for use.

LEGS: Hollywood jargon for a film that lasts at the box office. A film is said to "have legs" if it continues to draw crowds, week after week.

LOCATION: A site for shooting that is away from the studio (as in "on location").

LOOPING: The replacement of dialogue and other sounds on a film sound track. Quite often, actors re-record lines that weren't read properly on the set or needed to be changed due to technical problems, synchronizing them to a projection of the film footage. Also known as ADR (automatic dialogue replacement).

MASKING: The black borders around a movie screen. The borders can often be moved to accomodate various film aspect ratios.

MASTER SHOT: Similar to the "establishing shot," the master shot sets up the situations to which other scenes are related—often used first before close-ups of the conversations between actors. The master shot generally is filmed first, complete with all dialogue and actions. Individual head shots (one-shots or two-shots) are done separately with the same dialogue and actions, and then spliced in during the editing process to create scene continuity.

MATTE SHOTS: A matte is a specially-designed photographic mask which allows the "sandwiching" of one image into another—usually for special effects. In a matte shot, an actor may well be working on but a tiny portion of a scene; then the film is matted into a larger portion of film—usually a painted background. The

matte shot is generally used to create the illusion of great size and depth—or to overlay elaborate special effects devices. A "traveling matte" is a movable mask that allows movement from two different scenes to be integrated into one. In a "Blue Screen" matting process (chroma-key), the actors work in front of a blue background, which is dropped out during final assembly and replaced with a background from another locale.

M.O.S.: Shooting without an accompanying sound track. Legend has it that the term derives from "mit out sound," used by German director Lothar Mendes.

NUT: The amount of money a movie theater has to make to cover its operating costs. If the movie doesn't draw large enough crowds, the theater may not "make its nut."

ONE-SHOT: A picture of one person on the screen; a close-up of two people is a TWO-SHOT.

OPEN WIDE: No, it's not dialogue from a dentist, or whatever obscene connotation you just conjured up. When a film "opens wide," it is simulataneously released to theaters across the country. See also PLATFORM.

OVER THE SHOULDER: A shot taken from over the shoulder of one actor usually looking toward another. But it can also be used to establish the character's point of view.

PAN & SCAN: Adapting of a rectangular motion picture film to a relatively square television format. The television picture uses approximately two-thirds of the film image.

PLATFORM: A film releasing technique where a movie is released first in major cities, then as the box-office and publicity momentum build up, is then opened in smaller and smaller cities. The opposite of "opening wide."

PLOT: The main story line of a film; a "plot point" is something that happens during the unfolding of the story to turn the action toward a particular direction.

POINT OF VIEW (POV): In essence, what would be seen through an actor's eyes in his or her point of view. This is duplicated by the camera to give the audience the same point of view.

PRODUCER: Think of the producer as the Chief Executive on a particular film project. The producer usually instigates the film project, hires the writers and supervises script development, arranges for the financing, and generally manages the company that oversees the individual production. There's also an "Executive Producer," who, on quite a number of films, is merely somebody's brother-in-law.

PRODUCTION VALUES: The sum total of generally intangible factors contributing to the quality of a motion picture, or the lack thereof. Production values, as established by the film's budget, range from the quality of the people who work on the set to the costumes, scenery, art direction, and the like.

PROP: Any movable item—other than furniture—that is used on the set and in the scene. "Hand props" are the items that actors actually carry—ranging from guns to bouquets. The props are managed by the Property Master.

PROJECTION PLATE: Usually a slide which is projected onto a background to create a scene. On some sets, screens cover exterior windows and projection plates are used to create the scene that might be seen through the window.

REVERSE: A shot taken from an angle approximately 180 degrees from the preceding one. Normally used in a scene involving a two-actor conversation or entry through a doorway.

RF MIKE: A wireless microphone, also known as a "radio frequency" mike. The RF mike is worn by the actor, and a transmitter hidden in the clothing transmits back to the sound record equipment.

SAG: No, we're not talking about the dropping of body parts. SAG is Hollywoodese for the Screen Actors Guild, the union that represents actors. Having a "SAG Card" means that you're a member of the union. See also TAFT-HARTLEY.

SCENE: A division of the film's action—usually, that which takes place at a single location. Can be one shot or a series.

SCREEN DIRECTION: Movement of an actor or an object (train, car, etc.) from one side of the screen to another. If a car exits from one side of the screen (the right, for example), in the next shot it should enter from the left side to avoid jarring the viewer.

SWEETENING: Improving the sound track by removing extraneous noise, as well as adding extra sound and audio effects (such as reverberation) to enhance the sound quality. In television, "sweetening" also includes adding the laugh track, even though this is rarely done in films.

TAFT-HARTLEY: A labor law that permits an actor to work non-union for thirty days before being required to join the union (usually SAG or AFTRA). After the first thirty days, you're said to be "Taft-Hartleyed" and are then eleigible to join the union.

THE MONEY IS ON THE SCREEN: An expensive film that looks expensive. Especially as applied to movies that are heavy with well-realized special effects, if "the money is on the screen," it means that you're seeing the results of some massive expenditures. In essence, it's "what you see is what you get."

WRAP: As in "wrap-up," when a scene or a film is wrapped, it is completed—thus, the term "it's a wrap" frequently heard on the set…or "are we wrapped?" often asked by actors and technicians ready to head home for the day.

This glossary is a wrap.

THE SHARP-EYED, QUICK-WITTED FILM FLUBS SPOTTER SQUAD

Bill Adams, N. M. Almason, Nicole Almond, Gregory Aloia, Bart Andrews, Marilyn Andrews, Farnaz Arbabi, Kent Arney, Victor J. Arone, Lee Arrasmith, Bill Baker, Robert Barnett III, Joseph Barrus, R. Bergen, Douglas A. Berlin, Eric Berlin, Michael Bifulco, James Bilbro, Robert E. Blades, Andrew Blank, Nancy Blevins, Ken Bollin, Damian Bonito, Hal Bornkamp, Joy Boysen, Sarah E. Boyer, Michael A. Bragg, Steve Brattlie, Jack Bright, Rosemary Breslin, Kevin R. Brogan, Corey Brunish, Scott N. Buel, Steve Burks, William A. Callis, Janet Canizaro, Chris Carnicelli, C. Carroll, Steven Case, Stephen Chappell, Lou Charlip, Remy Chevalier, C. Dean Chu, James Clink, Bill Coberly, Adele Cohen, Glen Colton, Mike Concialdi, Tom Condo, Karla Conrad, Mark Conrath, Terry Copeland, Bill Cotter, Dick Councilman, Stephen L. Cox, Gary Crowell, Kimball Crum, Rory Cunningham, Gary Czosek.

Jennifer Davidoff, Alex deFrancisco, Marc DeLeon, Helen L. De-Zwarte, Roger DeKraker, David DiGiovanni, Tammi Dillhoff, Brian Dippie, Glenda Dixon, Margo Donohue, Jim Doran, Vince Dougherty, Kemper B. Durand, Wendy Eaton, Rachel Eberts, Diana Egan, Rob Eigenbrod, Steve Elmendorf, Tom Elmore, Mike Ensing, Rev. William J. Federer S.J., Joan Fedje, Jeff Felderman, Kevin Fellman, Sharon Fentiman, James Ferazzi, Larry Fisher, H. Fisher, Carol Fitzgibbons, Lance K. Fletcher, Daniel H. Flye, Jr., Chris and Dianne Fogus, Mark Foster, George T. Fox, Jim Fox, Deb'y S. Gaj, Jim Gates, Denise Garofalo, Donna Geeslin, Patrick Geoghegan, George George, Anthony Gesamondo Jr., Rev. Francis Gillespie, E. Glenesk, Linda Gnat-Mullin, Lee Goldberg, R. C. Graybeal, Julynne Greaves, R. Greco, Jr., Karen & Nelson Green, James M. Grout, John Hagen-Brenner, Jim Halacz, David Haley, Stuart E. Hallett, Jr., Rickey L. Hammon, David C. Harrison, Ruth Hayler, Bobby Newton Hendrix, Jr., Allah Hirsh, Joe Hoechner, Dan Hollombe, Jo Holmes, Kim Hoover, Jack Hoover, Candee Hopkins, William H. Hotaling, Brad Hurtado, Daryle L. Jenkins, Eric N. Jensen, Ted Jarasik, Andy D. Jimenez, Clint Johnson, Susan M. Johnson, Mark A. Johnson, H. J. Jones, Patrick Jordan, Terry Julian, Ted Jurasik.

Kirsten Kaffine, Ralph T. Kam, Glenn Kay, Dan Kelso, Gregory Kirschling, Brian Klug, John Kobal, Mary Ann Kobbs, Mitch Kramer, Phil Kulka, Dave Lechance, Alan David Laska, Nicole Lawlor, Andrea Lehrer, Jack E. Leonard, Donna Leonard-Dubinsky, Richard Lewis

Anthony Li Bruzzi, Mitchell Lindgren, Charles B. Lilly, Phil Lisa, Paul M. Lisnek, Ray Lombard, Margorie Loring, Sidney S. Louis, Debi Lovell, M. Llewellyn, Nancy Lucido, Bryan Luedeke, Mitchell Lundgren, Christine & Craig Mallon, Michael Mallory, Carolyn H. Malone, Leonard Maltin, Charlotte Manes, Michael Mann, Dave Mann, Michael Marks, Phil Marsh, Carman Marshall, Alvin H. Marill, Terri L. Marroquin, Wendy McArdle, Stephen C. McCracken, Judy McLaughlin McGinnis, James McGlynn, Jim McGrath, Tracey Caryl McIntire, Rob Medich, Harry Medved, Michael Medved, John Merli, Laura M. Miller, Joe Miller, Bob Miller, John Miller, Laura M. Miller, Terri Minsky, Peter J. Mones, John P. Morrett, Carolyn Mullins, J. A. Munson, Rebecca Naseck, Paul Natale, Richard Nayer, Robert Nelson, Nancy Nemeck, John Newton, Wayne Norman, Jed Novak, Curly O'Leary, Dianna Oldson, Pete Pallatta, Marianne Pannwitz, Bob Parker, Josh Parker, John E. Parnum, Kimberly S. Parr, Steve Paullus, Frank Paulson, Esq., Mary K. Payne, Pam Perkins, John Peterson, Mark Petty, Sue Phalen, Craig Phillips, Connie Picker, Jim Pinkston, Yolanda M. Pizarro, Lynne Poindexter-Garrett, Gregg Porter, Monty L. Preiser, Phyllis Puryear, Michael M. Pusich.

Moral Quest, Mildred Randon-Ramirez, Rolf Rathman, Max Reagan, Mike Reynolds, William E. Richardson, Bradley Richman, Col. Nick Riggs, Bridget Riley, Hilary Roberts, Kristy Rodriguez, Chris Rojahn, Miles J. Rudisill, Mildred Rondon-Ramirez, John J. Russo, Steven L. Sachs, Andrew Saidi, Bob Sandler, Rick Schatz, Steve Scheer, Amy Schell, Nat Segaloff, John Sekara, Bill Short, Ed Sikov, Wayne Simmons, Sandra Skoda, Bill Slattery, Fred Sliter, Mary Ellen Snodgrass, Joe Sonderman, Thomas S. Spiegel, Sandee St. John, Jeff Starkey, Kingsley Stevenson, Robert Stewart, Bill H. Stiles, Bryan Stoneburner, Lee Strauss, Dave Strauss, Howard Sudnow, D. J. Sule, Bernard J. Sussman, Steve Swedenburg, Lov Szymanski, Del Thiessen, Jack Thompson, Helen Thompson, Jim Trapp, Jon Trask, Jaye Ulmer, Jennifer Urcioli, Peter Van Gelder, Sam Waas, George Walden, Alex Ward, Bill Warren, A. L. Waters, Ken Watson, Bill Watson, Mary Wehrheim, Lisa Wehrlie, Corey Wells, Rena J. Welsh, Tom Wengerski, Patrick Whalen, Patricia Wiley, Jerry E. Willingham, Chris Willman, Norman Wilner, Kelly A. Wolfe, Alex Wolff, Henry Wong, Heather Zeigler, J. P. Zito

Sources

Movie Anecdotes by·Peter Hay. Oxford University Press, New York, 1990

That's Hollywood by Peter Van Gelder. Harper Perennial, New York, 1990

Roger Ebert's Movie Home Companion by Roger Ebert. Andrews & McMeel, Kansas City, Mo., 1990

Movie Clips by Patrick Robertson. Guinness Superlatives, Endfield, Middlesex, 1989

Hollywood Anecdotes by Paul F. Boller, Jr., and Ronald L. Davis. Ballantine Books, New York, 1988

Leonard Maltin's TV Movies and Video Guide by Leonard Maltin. New American Library, New York, 1991

The Man in Lincoln's Nose by Melinda Corey and George Ochoa. Simon & Schuster, New York, 1990

Continuity in Film and Video by Avril Rowlands. Focal Press, Stoneham, Mass., 1989

The Filmmaker's Handbook by Edward Pincus and Steven Ascher. New American Library, New York, 1984

"No Kidding"; World Features Syndicate

"Miss Takes" by Dave Strauss. Los Angeles *Daily News,* October 12, 1983

"Keep Your Eyes on the Screen" by Dave Strauss. New York *Daily News,* July 31, 1983

"Not Quite Ready When You Are, C. B." by John Kobal. *Esquire,* April 1969

"Movie Mistakes Fun to Follow" by Rosemary Breslin. New York *Daily News,* March 15, 1986

"Gotcha! Mistakes the Moviemakers Missed" by Susan Wloszczyna. *USA Today,* December 6, 1990

"Private Parts" by Susan Clabon-Rutland. *Movieline,* June 1991

TITLE INDEX